Praise for Sally J. Smith & Jean Steffens

STEALING THE GOLDEN DREAM

"*Stealing the Golden Dream* is a worthy follow-up to *Stealing the Moon and Stars*. A great series and smart plot told at breakneck pace with a fair share of red herrings thrown in to keep the brain busy. Eddie and Jordan are great characters, sexy, tough, intelligent, and witty. The saying that opposites attract is a perfect description of their relationship. They are supported by a terrific cast of villains and heroes, and the great landscape of Arizona thrown in for good measure adds extra weight to the enjoyment and thrill. *Stealing the Golden Dream* is the perfect companion for the beach, planes, trains and everything else in between."
—Sam Millar, The New York Journal of Books

"Smart and sassy. Classy with a twist of wry humor and just enough sentiment and romance to reel you in and keep you hanging until the end. Smith and Steffens, partners in crime-writing fiction, have struck gold again in *Stealing the Golden Dream*. Their characters are so engaging and real, you'll want to hire them next time you need a good PI team."
—Kathleen M. Rodgers, author of *Johnnie Come Lately* and *The Final Salute*

"The Smith and Steffens dynamic duo have created another enjoyable read. Blending their contemporary noir heroes with their quirky and relatable friends and relatives, followed by a generous sprinkling of really scary bad guys, this tight story tingles with suspense, grit, and perpetual motion. Living in Phoenix, I enjoyed the sense of place they created that portrays the unique character of the Phoenix and Scottsdale community. If you enjoy romantic suspense, you will love this book."

—Cathy Ann Rogers, author of *Here Lies Buried* and *Deliberate Fools*

"Jordan Welsh and Eddie Marino are an engaging duo, reminiscent of Castle and Beckett. Their chemistry makes this a must-read series. Smith and Steffens pen a heck of an action-packed, twisty-turny tale—they had me from page one!"

—Jenn McKinlay, *New York Times* best-selling author

STEALING THE MOON & STARS

"A sassy maverick heiress and a sexy good guy making amends for his bad guy past form a dynamite PI team in this promising debut from Sally J. Smith and Jean Steffens. A fun, romantic read, *Stealing the Moon & Stars* will keep you engaged all the way through its action-packed climax, and make you wish for the next book in the series. A winner!"

—Kris Neri, author of *Revenge on Route 66* and *Magical Alienation*

"With an action-packed, tightly crafted puzzler of a plot, *Stealing the Moon & Stars* is an impossible book to put down. Smith and Steffens have created delightful characters in Jordan Welsh and Eddie Marino that keep the reader laughing as well as shouting out warnings. Jordan and Eddie are the best mystery solving duo since Nick and Nora. Is there a fire alarm ringing? Because their relationship is smokin' hot!"

—Jenn McKinlay, *New York Times* bestselling author of the Cupcake Bakery Mysteries and the Library Lover's Mysteries

"The action and sexual tension are as hot as an Arizona summer. The Shea Investigations team put their lives, and their hearts, on the line in this action-packed crime novel."
—Lesa Holstine, Lesa's Book Critiques

"Take a private investigator who is one smart, independent lady, add a sexy business partner with a mysterious and none-too-savory past, throw in a dash of embezzlement, a dollop of betrayal, and a pinch of organized crime, and it all equals a suspenseful and witty tale that will keep you reading way past your bedtime."
—Donis Casey, author of the Alafair Tucker Mysteries

"Smith and Steffens is the team to watch or better yet, the team to read. *Stealing the Moon & Stars* is a smooth and clever story. But don't get too comfortable because it is also a well-crafted, suspenseful ride with unexpected twists and riveting characters. By the way, hands off. I have dibs on Eddie."
—Maria Grazia Swan, best-selling author of *Mina's Adventures* and the Lella York Series.

"The romantic/sexual tension between Jordan and Eddie is palpable, but it doesn't detract from the story at all. *Stealing the Moon & Stars* is an excellent start to a brand new series with a straightforward mystery and compelling characters."
—The Bibliophilic Book Blog

"Enjoyed it so much it was hard to put down. Got caught up in the investigations and the love affair .... Quite a few surprises that take everyone for a turn. Throw in a mix of family members and you got a good read. Light romance and sex but enough to help move the story along and it's the forbidden love that will make this series continue as they work together on more cases."
—Julie Barrett's Blog

"This is a great, lighthearted read. I highly recommend it for those readers who like PI, mystery and light romance!"
—Hily's Beehive

"If you enjoy a fast paced romance, this will fill the bill. Add suspense and spice and you have a romantic suspense with a bit of a twist. If you are in the market for a great beach or escape reading experience then this is the work for you. It seems that we may have a new dynamic duo in private investigations."
—Leslie Ann Wright, TicToc Reviews

"Their romance certainly had my heart pounding, and I can't wait to see how their relationship evolves in book two, especially since Jordan's left wondering if he's being completely honest with her about his actions. But throwing more obstacles in their way only seems to bring these two closer together."
—Connie Char, The Character Connection

"It was a treat reading about warm and sunny Arizona while toiling through an extremely long and cold winter. Between the desert heat and the sparks flying off of Jordan and Eddie, this book definitely made me feel all tingly inside."
—City Girl Who Loves to Read

"I found this to be an adventure filled romp, sometimes a dangerous endeavor when it comes to solving this crime. As the investigation goes on, you are taken deeper into the mystery of it all. Smith and Steffens keep you guessing at every turn. If you like a thrilling suspense novel with a steamy romantic twist, you will definitely enjoy this book."
—Tribute Books Mama

Stealing the Golden Dream

Stealing the Golden Dream

A Jordan Welsh & Eddie Marino Novel

Sally J. Smith
and
Jean Steffens

Seattle, WA

Camel Press
PO Box 70515
Seattle, WA 98127

For more information go to: www.Camelpress.com
www.smithandsteffens.com

Cover design by Sabrina Sun

Stealing the Golden Dream
Copyright © 2015 by Sally J. Smith and Jean Steffens

ISBN: 978-1-60381-985-5 (Trade Paper)
ISBN: 978-1-60381-986-2 (eBook)

Library of Congress Control Number: 2015931884

Printed in the United States of America

Acknowledgments

~

THE AUTHORS WISH TO thank Mike Steffens for his extensive research on the Dahlonega Mint and the limited edition coins minted there, also for his assistance regarding pharmaceutical matters. Thanks, Mike! ☺

Chapter 1

As Eddie Marino made his way to the back of the museum building, Muggs's voice followed him. "Better get your jacket, boss. A little chilly out there. Or maybe Jordan will keep you warm tonight."

Eddie looked over his shoulder at his friend and employee sitting at the front desk, adjusting his chair and settling in for his shift.

"I should be so lucky," Eddie said.

"Sure," Muggs said. "Like you're not?"

"Knock it off." But Eddie snagged his bomber jacket from a locker and shrugged into it anyway.

Instead of taking the direct path back to the museum's reception area, he detoured through the exhibit room where the Golden Dream Dahlonega Collection was on display. The premium collection of gold coins was the reason Shea Investigations had been hired by the Arizona Heritage Museum, one of the star attractions in downtown Scottsdale.

I just don't get what all the fuss is about.

He leaned over one of the display cases and whistled long and low.

So that's what five and a half million worth of gold coins looks like.

He'd already skimmed over the promotional brochure, but only because his partner, the incomparable Jordan Welsh, had made him. The limited edition gold coins were minted between 1838 and 1861 in Dahlonega, Georgia, in varying denominations. Each complete set in the Golden Dream private collection was more pristine than the next. The collection was world famous, said to be the most complete in existence.

Lady Liberty looked good in gold—but five million plus? No wonder the museum hired extra protection while they had custody of the coins. A guy could buy a lot of toys with a chunk of change that size.

He made his way back out to the security desk and laid his hand on Muggs's shoulder. Muggs, indeed. His friend had been tagged with the ironic nickname back on the mean streets of Cleveland when the two were boyhood friends. It stuck. Marvin "Muggs" Baxter took a lot of good-natured ribbing because of his Hollywood golden boy looks. He was good people, always ready to step in when needed, always the one who had your back.

"Thanks for trading shifts with me, bro," Eddie said. "You saved my bacon. I promised Jordan I'd make the scene at this charity deal. Unfortunately." Truth be told, Eddie would much rather be spending this cool March evening curled up on the sofa beside Jordan with a good single malt and Coltrane in the background instead of prancing around in a monkey suit. He didn't mesh with most of the people who went to these charity events, and as a general rule they didn't get him either. But he didn't really care what the society crowd thought of him. This was for Jordan.

A lot of what he did these days was for Jordan, but that was the way it was supposed to be. Wasn't it? Once you found *the one*, you hung your future on her. Jordan's happiness and well being meant everything to him, and she didn't ask him to show up at these stuffy shindigs very often. It was the least he could do. Jordan—beautiful, stubborn, independent as hell Jordan. He realized he was smiling.

Ah, what the hell. Maybe their old clients Nick and Connie Brenner would show up. At least he'd have something to talk to them about.

Muggs stood and moved out from behind the desk. "I don't mind switching. Glad to." He hesitated. "You got a minute before you leave?"

"Sure," Eddie said. "What's up?"

"It's my dad. I just found out he's pretty sick."

"Sick? Sick how?"

"Sick like on a clock, you know? Short time. They gave my old man an expiration date. Does that suck or what? He's my dad, for crying out loud, not a carton of milk. Three to six months." Muggs's voice broke from emotion.

Eddie's heart went out to his friend. Old man Baxter. When Eddie's own father was killed in a riot at a Cleveland dock strike, Muggs's father had held Eddie when he couldn't keep the pain inside anymore and wept until he was so spent he shuddered. And how many times had he gone to Muggs's dad with those questions a teenage boy can only ask a man?

Within the circle of the trio Eddie called his crew—Tank, Diego, and Muggs—Muggs had always been the family guy, the one who called his folks every weekend and flew home four times a year. "Aw, man, I'm so sorry. That just blows. Your dad's a really good guy. I always liked him."

"So, I was thinking of taking some time off, if it's okay. You know, to be there. With him. With Mom. She's gonna need somebody, too."

"Of course. No problem." Eddie laid his hand on Muggs's shoulder. "You didn't even have to ask. Take whatever time you need. We got you."

"Thanks. I'd like to leave for Cleveland as soon as possible— spend every minute I can with him before … you know."

"Absolutely. When you know your schedule, give a shout. I'll be your ride to the airport. And if you need me back there, you'll let me know. Right?"

Muggs nodded and looked away. He cleared his throat. "Anything I should know about this gig before you leave?"

"Nope. I just checked on their fancy coin collection. It's all good. Copacetic."

Muggs followed Eddie to the door. "I'll lock up behind you."

Eddie circled once around the one-story brick building through the alley. Everything looked tight as a drum. Yep, this was Scottsdale, all right. You couldn't even really call the area behind the museum an alley. It was a wide space with half a dozen or so parking spots marked off. Clean and free of debris and the sort of alley clutter you'd find in most cities. Brightly lit. Noise carried from a couple of blocks east where the Old Town nightclub district would just be gearing up. It was a scene he'd been into once, but not for a while, not since Jordan.

He went around the building to the side of the museum where his car was parked on Marshal Way. A mini-tram driver slumped behind the wheel catching a snooze before he began a night's work of shuttling partiers from gin joint to gin joint. A couple of spaces over from the tram sat Eddie's sweet little ride, a black 2006 Porsche Boxster convertible. Before getting in, he hit the lock release on his key fob and ran his hand affectionately along the fender.

It was barely seven o'clock. He had just enough time to swing by his place, change into a tux, and pick up Jordan at eight—that is if he stepped on the Boxster and stayed out of the way of Scottsdale's finest.

This job for the Arizona Heritage Museum was sweet, the kind he wished Shea Investigations could snag every day of the week. Easy money, especially when you compared it to the grinding-it-out donkeywork the firm had to take when they first started out.

Eddie and Jordan Welsh had joined forces to form their

security and private investigation agency ten months earlier—and who would have thunk it? Shea Investigations quickly became one of the best damn firms in Scottsdale. That was partly thanks to the success of a big case they handled the previous fall for The Moon & Stars Foundation. In Eddie's vernacular, that case gave Eddie and Jordan seats at the grownups' table.

These days, except for the favored client here and there, they didn't have to fool around with skip traces, background checks, and stray husband surveillance. He pulled out of the parking spot and turned the Boxster east on Fifth Avenue toward Scottsdale Road.

Gotta admit though, sometimes I do miss seeing that flabbergasted look on the face of some poor wayward sap when he gets a load of him and his Friday night girl rolling around under the sheets on video.

EDDIE PULLED INTO THE driveway of Jordan's house in North Scottsdale. The coach lights by the garage doors and front entrance cast a warm glow over the terracotta, Mediterranean-style architecture. Strategically placed ground lights illuminated the lone saguaro in the yard as well as the small cluster of mesquite trees shading her den when the morning sun climbed over the McDowell Mountains.

It was a really nice place—not quite as upscale as one would expect from an old-moneyed trust fund baby like Jordan. She saved up the downstroke on her own, and the mortgage payments were made from her agency income. It was a source of pride to Jordan and frustration to her mother, who just didn't understand why her youngest daughter wanted to fend for herself as much as possible. No matter what her mother thought, Jordan's house was still a really nice place to live, even if it felt like playing house when he stayed over.

He compared Jordan's suburban lifestyle to the sleek high-rise city condo and more urban way of life he'd chosen. Her neighborhood just wasn't his bag—a little too Wisteria Lane for him. He was a city boy all the way.

He glanced at the dash. Eight o'clock on the nose. He moved up the walkway and rang the bell.

Jordan yanked open the door. "I'm not quite ready."

Quite ready? She stood there in a lacy, lilac teddy almost covering her luscious personality. Her cheeks were flushed, her voice breathless. *Hubba-hubba.* "I can see that, babe," Eddie said. God, she was a knockout. He cleared his throat, but his voice was still higher-pitched than normal. "Maybe we should just stay in tonight."

He reached for her, but she danced away just beyond his grasp.

"Not tonight. You promised we'd go. Okay, so rubbing elbows with Scottsdale hoity-toities isn't your favorite pastime, but it's for a good cause. Plus, making an appearance at these things is good for business. We won't stay long. I promise."

He growled, "Yeah. Yeah. But you also gotta promise I'll get another look at that outfit later on."

He followed her in and took a seat on the sofa. Jordan's pampered golden retriever, Sadie, pounced on him. *Great! Dog hair. Just what I need.*

Jordan had said Sadie had a massive crush on him. He rubbed her behind the ears—Sadie, not Jordan—and smiled when she rolled her eyes and turned to mush under his hand. Now that he thought about it, it might not be such a bad idea to try the ear-rubbing thing on Jordan.

Inside of fifteen minutes, Jordan walked out of her bedroom wearing a slinky little black dress and a pair of five-story heels showing off her exquisite legs. She only wore those shoes when she was with him.

On more than one occasion she said, "I don't look like an amazon when I wear stilettos with you. You're taller than I am."

How could a woman as stunning as she be concerned about her height? She wasn't just tall, she was statuesque.

Magnificent—in his book anyway. Her issue with it was one of the mysteries of Jordan.

He was carried back almost a year and a half to the first time he laid eyes on her. In fact, he'd laid more than just his eyes on her. He'd tackled her and pinned her to the floor at a warehouse job they were working under separate employment contracts. Even in that awkward moment, something about her went straight to his heart. He'd been so taken with her when she approached him ten months ago to merge his security company with her JW Investigations, he didn't hesitate long enough to consider the profitability factor. But, hey, it had worked out great in the end, so no harm, no foul.

Tonight, *his* woman—as he'd come to think of Jordan but would never put it that way to her—looked nothing short of spectacular, although in his opinion, she still wore way too many clothes.

"You look hot tonight," she said, vocalizing the compliment he'd mentally paid her. "Let's go, Marino."

Her phone rang. It was Mary Welsh's ringtone, the "Imperial March"—Darth Vader's theme. Jordan looked at Eddie. Eddie looked at Jordan. She mouthed, "Mother."

He mouthed, "I know," and shook his head.

She shrugged apologetically as she slid her finger over the screen. "Mom. What's up? Eddie says, 'Hi.'"

Eddie whispered, "No, I didn't."

Mary Welsh's shrill voice came over the speaker. "Oh, Jordan, I've done a terrible thing. Somehow I managed to miss the bottom step off the rear patio. I hurt myself."

"Mom. Hurt? How hurt?"

"My ankle. It's excruciating. Do you think you could take me to the hospital?"

Swell. Eddie watched his chance for a second peek at the lilac teddy fly out the window.

"Where's Daddy?"

"Chicago. The lease on our Welsh's Steak and Chop House on Superior is up for renegotiation. You know how your dad loves wheeling and dealing. Thinks he's such a shark and nobody else can take care of the family business quite the way he can. He went a couple of days ago."

"Alec?" Jordan asked.

"Your brother's at the Scottsdale steakhouse. It's spring training season, and we are busy, busy, busy. Where else would the manager be? Working, of course. Isn't that what the Welsh men always seem to be doing?"

"And you couldn't reach anyone else?"

Eddie could see she was running out of options.

"I tried Katie, but your sister didn't pick up the call." Mary sighed. "My guess? She's out hiking some mountain with that cuddly man of hers. They're too adorable together. I'm thinking nuptials within the next year or two. It'll be nice having a bank president in the family."

"Dave's the manager of the bank, Mom, not the president."

"Whatever," Mary said. "Kate might be working late at the crisis center." Frustration laced her voice. "Millions of dollars in trust funds for you kids, and you're all always off working somewhere. What good is being wealthy if it doesn't free up your time so you can take care of your mother?"

Jordan rolled her eyes. Eddie had to admit she held no illusions about her mother. Mary Welsh was a card-carrying narcissist and could be a full-blown bitch when she wanted to be. *But, hey, nobody's perfect.*

"Jordie? Please. It hurts."

Jordan deflated right in front of him and turned apologetic hazel eyes his way. "I'll be right there, Mom." She hung up, reached in her bag, and took out her keys.

He stood. "Toss me the keys. I'll drive."

"What? And ruin both our evenings? No. I'll go get her. I'm giving you a pass on the fundraiser, Marino, but I'll take a rain check." She paused. "Seriously, I don't like going to those things any more than you do, but if it's a good cause, it's worth it."

"Nothing beats a good cause." He almost meant it.

He kissed her good night and grabbed a handful of her sweet bottom before heading to his car with a spring in his step. Reprieve from the stuffed shirt affair—but not a total win. He'd been totally looking forward to getting Jordan out of the cute little teddy. There'd be another time. Sooner than later, if he had his way.

JUST BEFORE SIX, THURSDAY morning, Eddie turned off Scottsdale road onto Fifth Avenue and nearly took out a half-dozen sunburned college students stumbling across the street. From the look of them, they were just now heading to their hotel after a night of carousing in the downtown club district. Every spring break in the Valley of the Sun brought more party kids than the year before.

He returned his attention to Jordan's call. "Glad to hear Mary Mary Quite Contrary is okay. Guess she'll live to dance at another charity ball."

Eddie wasn't just being polite. He really was glad to hear Mary Welsh wasn't badly hurt. Head over heels crazy about Jordan meant a certain level of commitment, and her family was part of the deal. But the Welshes weren't exactly an easy A. As gorgeous as they all were, they still had a lot of warts, and Mary Welsh a few more than the rest of them—if you asked him anyway. She'd made it quite clear the way she saw it: he was okay in her book as long as he wasn't happily-ever-after for her well-heeled daughter. Mary was good old American steel under that sleek exterior, but he doubted her resolve could stand up to his. He wasn't going anywhere.

"They X-rayed," Jordan said. "Just a bad sprain. She flirted outrageously with all the doctors at the ER. It was mortifying. Thank God, Dad will be home tonight to assume nursing duties. Do you and the crew need me to take a shift at the museum? If not, I'll hook up with Steve Keegan. He wants to meet at the Jokers Wild nightclub down south to touch base with the Phoenix PD Arson Division people."

"Give Keegan my regards. You don't need to take a shift at the museum. We should be able to … hey, what's this?"

Parked on the street up ahead outside the Arizona Heritage Museum were enough emergency vehicles to man the entire first response team of a small city. "I gotta go, babe."

"Eddie, what?"

"I just gotta go."

He accelerated up the block, rounded the iconic Bob Parks Bronze Horse Fountain and skidded to a stop. He threw open the car door, leapt out, and ran into the building.

A Scottsdale uniformed cop inside the door grabbed him by the arm and yanked him around. "Hey, man. You can't go in there. This is a crime scene."

Eddie jerked away and stopped just short of clocking the cop.

"It's okay, Officer," Detective Ann Murphy called from across the room. "I know this man. I'll talk to him."

"What's going on?" Eddie asked.

The Scottsdale Police detective had been Jordan's friend for a couple of years now, and lately the two women had grown close. Ann's usually unlined face looked tired—more than tired. Exhausted. Disheartened. She ran her hand through her short blonde hair. Her shoulders slumped. "Eddie, you better sit down."

Chapter 2

⌒

EDDIE HELD HIS HEAD in his hands and didn't look up when Jordan walked in. He sat on a bench in the same room where the coin collection had been displayed. It wasn't there anymore. A scuffle at the center of the room caught her attention. Tank and Diego, two-thirds of Eddie's crack team, were trying to strong-arm their way through a cluster of police and medical personnel. The police did a fair job of keeping them outside the circle.

Eddie was clearly suffering and not in the mood for company. She crossed to where Ann Murphy and her partner, Detective Neil Thompson, stood with the county medical examiner.

The body was visible now. She didn't mean to look, didn't want to, but couldn't help herself.

Muggs lay on his back. The blood pooled beneath him on the slick travertine had soaked into his signature Hawaiian print shirt. His long blond hair was matted with it. His handsome face was frozen in a grimace, and it was no wonder. The vicious knife wound ran from his gut to his breastbone. Why would somebody do such a thing?

The whimper she'd tried so hard to hold in slipped out.

Her throat closed up but not from nausea, from nearly unbearable emotion. "I'm so sorry, baby." Her voice was as raw as her pain.

"Looks personal, doesn't it?" Ann said from behind her.

Jordan turned from the body. "Personal? Nobody hated Muggs, certainly not enough to want him dead. The man had no enemies." She added, "Thanks for calling me, Ann."

"When I saw how hard Eddie was taking it, I knew he needed you."

Jordan glanced over at her partner, her lover. His closed-in posture was a study in devastation.

"And those two?" Past the archway, Tank and Diego were ushered to the front door where they waited. Their barely contained grief and rage radiated from every pore.

Ann shook her head. "God help the man who did this if those two get hold of him."

"What happened here?" Jordan asked.

Detective Thompson walked up, his long, mournful face as serious as ever, his tone sarcastic. "What does it look like? Someone robbed the place and killed your friend."

"Don't be a dick, Detective," Ann said.

"The coin collection in this room was worth over five million." Eddie's voice was barely audible. He stood and crossed the room to join them. He walked like an old man, his posture slumped, his gait labored.

"Hell, for five million I'd rob the place myself," the disgruntled detective grumbled.

Eddie's head came up. "If you killed one of my friends in the process then I'd have to come after you, just like I'm going after the son of a bitch who butchered Muggs." Not a threat or a promise—simple statement of fact.

Jordan recognized the look on Eddie's face. She'd seen it before. Lethal commitment. It frightened even her.

The lanky detective's Adam's apple bobbed as he swallowed hard, cleared his throat, and walked away.

One of the cops came to the archway and leaned in. "Detective Murphy, there's a man out front. Says he's the curator."

Ann nodded. "He's here to take inventory. Let him in. I'll be out to talk to him."

"Mind if I tag along?" Jordan asked.

"Okay, but remember, it's my interview," Ann warned.

Jordan turned and looked at Eddie. "Coming?" His attention focused across the room where the body bag was being loaded onto a gurney. His gaze followed the progress as his friend was wheeled out.

Jordan stepped in front of him. This shouldn't be his last memory of Muggs.

His eyes met hers. "I'm going with Muggs," he said. "Me and the boys. You know what I need."

She nodded. "I'll find out everything I can."

Eddie left. Diego and Tank followed him out as the young officer escorted a short, older man into the crime scene room.

Jordan followed behind the detective, who met him halfway and stuck out her hand. "Detective Ann Murphy."

They shook. "Sid Hunter, head curator here." His small brown eyes were filled with dismay as they took in the empty display cases. His gaze settled on the dark blood staining the shiny floor. He rubbed his hand over the sparse hair on his head. "Oh, my goodness gracious. I saw them wheeling out a body. Someone was killed?" He spoke with a thick Brooklyn accent.

Jordan stepped forward. "I'm Jordan Welsh, Mr. Hunter, of Shea Investigations and Security."

"Oh. The special hire, right? The Brenners had the trustees contract you for this exhibit."

"It was our man on duty here last night who died."

Sid shook his head—and shook it and shook it. "Terrible, terrible thing."

Ann broke in. "Mr. Hunter, please go over the area as thoroughly as possible. We need to know what's missing."

"No need to go over the room, Detective Murphy. I can tell you what's missing." His hand swept the cases in front of him. "Everything."

"Which was …?" Ann prompted.

"The exhibit was all first run, primo. There were seven sets of gold coins from the short-lived Dahlonega mint in Georgia. They were graded at an average sixty-seven out of seventy— higher than any other remaining Dahlonega pieces. It was the entire Golden Dream Collection. We had the dies on display, other paraphernalia, and quite a few individual coins and partial sets. Goodness gracious. I'll have to look them up to compile an accurate list." His gesture encompassed the dozen or more display cases. "You can see from the empty cabinets how extensive the collection was. The small individual sleeves each coin was packaged in would make it way too easy for someone to steal the coins once they got the displays open. The pictures tell the whole story."

He walked along the wall. The two women followed as Sid pointed to the framed prints of mining sites and old buildings. "They only minted at Dahlonega, Georgia, a few years. Pre-Civil War. Not many of the coins remain. It's why they're valued so dearly. And ah, they're not like any other U.S. coins you've ever seen. Just beautiful. Works of art really." He turned to Jordan. "Miss Welsh, the museum's board members have asked me to meet with them this evening. It would be helpful if you could attend as well."

"Of course," Jordan said.

After Sid Hunter retired to his office to catalogue the missing items, Ann made a detective's to-do list of her own. "Finish the forensics, including fingerprints. Make sure the scene's adequately photographed. Collect any other possible evidence. Interview all employees. Review the closed circuit tapes." She looked up at Jordan. "I forget anything?"

Jordan's eyes met Ann's. *Put a bullet in the monster.* But she only shrugged.

"Jordan." The determination in Ann's voice sent a clear message of commitment. She intended to work the hell out of the case. "We'll get to the bottom of this, and if I have anything to do with it, sooner not later."

LUPE'S CANTINA IN CENTRAL Phoenix had been Muggs's favorite sleazy dive. Over the years, he and Eddie, Tank, and Diego had tossed back more shots there than Jordan would like to admit. A good share of those shots went down tonight, according to Lupe anyway.

Jordan got the call to come and haul her men away around a quarter to six in the evening. They'd been drinking since they left the morgue around eleven a.m.

"I've been watching these *hombres* all day, and now it's time for them to go. Too much liquor. Too much sadness," Lupe said.

Lupe was obviously right, about everything. Jordan knew it the minute she walked in.

"Ya know," Eddie slurred. "I knew Muggs longer than you two. We were friends first. Always had my back. Loved that guy. Our golden boy. To Muggs."

They clicked glasses, downed the shots and poured another round from the nearly empty bottle of Herradura Selección Suprema.

Diego sniffled. "He was one hell of a Marine. Here's to Muggs." His smooth Latino features were a bit slack, courtesy of the tequila. His curly black hair stood up here and there as if he'd had his hands in it.

"To Muggs," Tank and Eddie repeated. Another clink of glasses and another shot bit the dust.

"From the halls of Monte-z-u-u-ma …" Diego began in a key Jordan didn't recognize. The others joined in.

Jordan sighed. Their misery tugged at her heart.

From the bar came, "Hey, you guys. Quiet down over there. We're trying to watch the game."

The trio was obviously not a big hit.

The singing stopped.

Tank stood, pulled back his shoulders, and flexed his impressive pecs. "You got something against the Marines? That's downright un-American." He looked like an inebriated pit bull.

"Pipe down, dammit." The guy's tone was even more annoyed.

Eddie, Tank, and Diego looked at one another. Jordan cringed at the glee and resolve on their faces.

Eddie stood, sort of, weaving so badly she doubted he'd stay upright for long.

"Why don't you come on over here and make us?" Eddie Marino, glib as ever.

Jordan sighed. *Perfect.*

It took less than a minute for the loud-mouthed sports fan and his buddies to be all over Eddie and the two remaining members of his crew. It was lucky the boys were all three sheets to the wind. They still put four over the bar and would have done more damage if the bouncer and six of his friends hadn't deposited them on the sidewalk.

Jordan collected them, managed to get all three loaded into her silver Pilot, and drove them to their separate homes.

THERE WAS NO WAY on God's green earth Jordan planned to let Eddie Marino anywhere near the museum board members. He was a loose cannon, and she didn't want any cannonballs ricocheting around while she labored to salvage the agency's reputation.

At seven fifteen Thursday evening, Jordan met Sid Hunter at the Paradise Valley residence of Sarah and Rachel Abromowitz, the aging spinster sisters who headed up the board of the Arizona Heritage Museum.

They lived in a sprawling, Frank Lloyd Wright-style house among the rolling foothills and narrow roadways of the primo real estate of Paradise Valley just west of central Scottsdale. Jordan admired the character and clean lines. Though it was, sadly, one of what had come to be called "tear-downs." The next time it changed hands, the lot would probably be razed to host a slick McMansion. Too bad.

Sarah Abromowitz came to the door in a glittery lounging gown and velvet slippers. Her dark hair was pulled up on top of her head in a tight knot. She wore minimal makeup—taupe eye shadow and a rust-colored lipstick. She was eighty-five if she was a day.

"Do come in, please." Her voice was husky, and she spoke slowly and distinctly.

She led them through the old but elegant residence to a rear patio. With the outdoor heaters and mini-buffet, it seemed to be set for a cocktail party rather than a business meeting. An enormous pitcher of martinis, complete with a saguaro cactus swizzle stick, was the main feature of the table. Jordan accepted a drink from Rachel, a near carbon copy of her sister only with hair the color of a Mexican sunset. Rachel appeared to be a few years younger than Sarah.

Sid Hunter hovered nervously on the edge of the patio. He was the hired help, ill at ease in the environment.

"Mr. Hunter. Miss Welsh." Rachel's accent, like Sarah's, sounded like Midwestern old money. Jordan recognized it from her mother's coffee klatches in the Lake Forest residence with other dames who helped her plan this or that society event.

Sid Hunter and Jordan sat side by side on a loveseat. The niceties took about fifteen minutes or so. No, they didn't care for *hors d'oeuvres*. No, they had better stick to one martini. And yes, such a marvelous house. It was obvious the two lovely women were lonely and grabbed at every chance to entertain.

"We're simply mortified at the turn of events down at the museum," Sarah said.

Rachel nodded, then said, "We've asked you here tonight to

beg you and your associates to follow through on this matter. The museum's reputation is at stake."

Jordan didn't miss the unspoken inference that Shea Investigations' reputation was at stake right alongside the museum's. "Of course." She hoped she sounded confident. "Rest assured. We've cleared our caseload and are assigning our entire staff to the recovery of the coin collection."

The two ladies looked at each other, nodded, smiled, and in tandem took a sip of their martinis.

Chapter 3

ON FRIDAY MORNING, JORDAN lay listening to Sadie snore softly at the foot of the bed. Outside the Arcadia door, the big Acacia tree in the backyard swayed with the breeze. Another beautiful, early spring morning in the Valley of the Sun, but a day, like all those in the future, which had dawned without Muggs Baxter. "Bad Boys" blared from her phone—that would be Detective Murphy calling. Maybe there was already a break in the case. She snatched up her cellphone.

"Annie, I'm here. You get something?"

She glanced at the clock. Seven thirty. Ann was really busting her hump on the case.

"I did, but you're not going to like it. You need to meet me at Eddie's place."

"Eddie's place?" Jordan was wide-awake. "What's going on?"

"Not over the phone," Ann said.

There was something strained and unfamiliar in Ann's voice that made Jordan nervous, something that sounded too much like police business.

"That sounds ominous." Jordan tried to lighten things up, but when Ann didn't respond, she said, "You've got me worried."

"Just get your butt down to Eddie's now." Ann hung up.

She had a really bad feeling. Her stomach churned in confirmation. What was up? There was only one way to find out. She jumped out of bed.

After a quick walk through the shower, she pulled her wet hair back with a tortoise clip then slid into a pair of skinny jeans, an indigo cotton boyfriend shirt her mother bought her at Barney's, and a pair of purple sneaks. A quick look in the mirror verified it was passable for SDG: shower, dress, go.

Due to rush hour traffic, it was over forty minutes later when Jordan rang Eddie's bell.

When he didn't answer, she banged on the door. Still nothing. She used her key and went inside.

The place looked just as she'd left it the night before, clean and tidy except for Eddie's clothes strewn across the sofa. She had gladly helped him shed those clothes. He was too drunk to do it himself or to do anything about the feelings he aroused in her, especially naked.

Eddie's condo was on the eighth floor of a high-rent building in the bustling North Scottsdale central corridor. It was sleek and modern, just like Eddie. And at the moment, it was tomb quiet. He must still be asleep. After last night, she wasn't surprised.

His bedroom was dim, his long, lean silhouette defined under the dove gray sheets they'd cuddled under during her sleepovers.

She stood back from the bed. "Marino, wake up." She knew better than to get too close. He might punch her lights out.

Eddie moaned and rolled over onto his back. "Jordan? Whatcha doing here? Is it morning?"

"Get up and get dressed. Ann's on her way."

"Here?" He sat straight up and grabbed his head. "*Madonn'*." He swung his legs out, and his feet hit the carpet. "I need coffee."

When he stood the sheet fell away. Her gaze took in his naked body, the sinewy lines of his strong legs, the hard planes of his torso. No man had the right to be so beautiful. She cleared her throat. "I'll make you a cup."

A few minutes later, he joined her in the kitchen wearing jeans, his signature black T-shirt, and a pair of moccasin loafers. Jordan slipped a pod into the coffeemaker and hit the button. The aroma of the rich Kenyan blend filled the condo.

He took the cup and inhaled the steam. "You don't know how bad I need this. Did Ann say what she had?"

"No. Just said to meet her here." Jordan reached into the fridge for the cream, trying to shake off the nerves his question kick-started.

The doorbell rang. Eddie sipped his coffee as he crossed the room and opened the door.

From the kitchen Jordan could see Ann in the hallway. She wore black gabardine slacks and a two-button blazer over a white cotton blouse with red Converse high-tops. It was her standard detective uniform.

"Come on in. You want some?" Eddie lifted his cup.

"No thanks." Even from across the room, it was easy to see Ann didn't look him in the eye. "Eddie, I hate this, but I have to ask you some questions."

Jordan came from the kitchen. *She's in professional mode, and she looks like hell. That's not good.* What did Ann want with Eddie?

"Questions? Sure, ask away." He seemed unruffled and sat on the leather sofa patting the empty spot beside him.

Jordan took it.

Ann sank into the cushions of the orange slouch chair from Copenhagen, the one Jordan hated. A small black notebook and pen appeared from Ann's pocket. "First of all, I need to know where you were Wednesday night."

"Wednesday?" Jordan asked. "The night of the break-in?"

Eddie sat up straighter. "Me? Where you going with this, Ann?"

It wasn't Ann who looked back at him, it was Detective Murphy. Jordan held her breath. The beginning of an interrogation if she ever heard one.

"I was with this tall drink of water." He glanced at Jordan.

Ann looked at Jordan for confirmation.

Jordan nodded. "He was."

Ann focused her attention back on Eddie. "Time frame?"

"Muggs relieved me about seven. I dropped by here and changed clothes then went straight to Jordan's. I was there by eight. Say, wait a minute. You don't think I …."

Ann uncrossed her legs and shifted around. She seemed antsy. "I have to ask these questions. I need to rule out everyone. Jordan, what time did he leave you?"

She opened her mouth to lie flat out, but stopped when Eddie put his hand on her arm.

"I left after a few minutes. Jordan's mother called and said she hurt herself. Jordan had to take her to the ER."

Jordan nodded grudgingly.

Ann shifted her gaze back to Eddie. "You didn't go with her?"

"No. I came home." There was a furrow between his dark brows.

"So, you were with her *maybe* twenty, thirty minutes at the most?"

"That's right," he said.

Jordan reached for his hand. She knew what was coming and held her breath, praying she was wrong.

"Interact with anyone, Eddie? Can anyone back you up on this?"

He shook his head slowly.

Jordan's stomach lurched. "Maybe you called Tank? Diego? Anybody?"

Eddie didn't answer. He was looking at Ann, his dark eyes probing, inquisitive.

Ann snapped her notebook closed. "You don't have an alibi."

Eddie set his jaw. His chin came up. "Just get to the point, Murphy. Say what you came to say."

"We got an anonymous call—a burner phone. A tip to search your Porsche."

"You what?" Eddie half rose.

It was Jordan's turn to be the calm one. She touched his leg, and he sat back.

His hands shot into the air. "I can't believe this. One of my best friends is dead. And they're looking at me for it?"

"Eddie," Jordan said. She hoped he read the silent message she sent him. *Hold it together.*

The doorbell rang.

Ann said, "That will be Neil."

Jordan went to the door. Her hands were shaking, and her legs felt wobbly.

Ann's partner, Detective Neil Thompson, walked in with a black leather satchel and plopped it on the coffee table.

Eddie looked fit to be tied. "Hey, that's my bag. You can't just—"

Neil slapped a folded paper onto the table. "It's a warrant, dude. Even you probably know what a search warrant is. All nice and legal."

"What the hell you doing searching my car?"

Neil spoke in his "just the facts" detective tone. "Making a case."

Eddie looked ready to knock the other man to the floor. Neil's smart mouth wasn't helping matters. Maybe Ann would keep things stable, but, no, she was focused on the black bag.

"Why aren't you out there looking for the guy who killed my friend?" Eddie spit out.

"Because," Neil Thompson made a big show of pulling on a pair of thin latex gloves, "we figure we already got the guy who did it, pretty boy." He opened the bag, reached in, and laid the contents out one by one—a small case with Eddie's lock-picking tools, a high intensity flashlight, a clean black T-shirt, and a small tool kit.

"And what do we have here?" Neil lifted two small evidence

bags from the satchel and spread them in front of Eddie.

Eddie stared. His breathing was shallow and rapid, his face a little flushed. It was obvious he was having a difficult time staying calm.

The clear bags contained two small acrylic sleeves, each with one of the stolen Dahlonega gold coins.

"I never saw—"

"Yeah, I bet." Neil reached in again and came out with a larger bag, this one holding a bloody Bowie knife. "And what about this, sunshine? Bet you never saw this either? Huh?"

Eddie sat back against the sofa, stone-faced. Jordan didn't have to ask. He was done talking. And it was a smart move. The bloody knife was his or exactly like his. She'd seen it before—last fall when they worked a case for the Moon & Stars Foundation.

Ann stood, glanced at Jordan then said, "Eddie Marino, you're under arrest for the murder of Marvin Baxter, also known as Muggs Baxter, and the burglary of the Arizona Heritage Museum. You have the right to remain …."

Detective Thompson cuffed Eddie while Ann Mirandized him.

"Ann," Jordan said. "This is a frame-up and you know it. Why would he go to all the trouble to steal the coins and then leave them in the car?"

"It's just two coins," Ann replied. "They might have been left behind by accident."

Eddie's eyes never left Jordan's as they took him by the arms and led him toward the door.

"Jordan?" One word sending a thousand messages.

She nodded. "I got you. Don't worry."

"What, me worry? You forget who you're talking to, sweetheart." His words were casual, but his eyes were troubled.

Chapter 4

~

THE DOOR CLOSED BEHIND them, and Jordan collapsed onto the soft leather sofa. She buried her head in her hands and sat crying, finally able to give in to her emotions.

How could Ann just up and arrest Eddie like some thug off the street?

She was surprised to find herself breathing hard; then it struck her. Ann had a job to do, a hard job. *Cut the girl some slack, Jordan.* At least Ann gave them the consideration of doing this in the privacy of his place, not cuffing him out on the street or at the office. This wasn't the first time, and it probably wouldn't be the last time their friendship and their professional relationship were at odds.

The phone played "Darth Vader's Theme." "Oh, great, Mother, just what I need," she said aloud. She took a deep breath. "Hello?"

Why did she answer it? She didn't want to talk to her mother. Did she?

"Jordie, I just wanted to keep you in the loop. I'm doing much better. The drugs are helping."

A sob caught in Jordan's throat.

"Are you crying? I said I was fine, dear. Don't worry."

"No, no, I'm glad you're better."

"But you are crying. Tell Mother what's wrong."

"It's Eddie. They arrested him, Mom. Took him downtown."

"Arrested. Our Eddie? But, why would—?"

Since when was he *our* Eddie? "For theft ... and murder." Jordan couldn't hold back any longer. It all came out at once, the sobbing, the shaking, the blubbering and sniffling. She told Mary everything, every last detail. She was surprised as hell that she wanted to, but even more amazed at Mary's reaction.

"Are they out of their minds? Poor Eddie!"

What? No recriminations, no I-told-you-sos?

"I feel just terrible about this." Mary sounded genuinely upset.

"Why should you feel terrible? You didn't have anything to do with it."

"If it hadn't been for me, he would have been with you, and the police would have known he didn't do it. It's all because of the darn step I fell off. I'm going to have that deck ripped out!"

Not about you this time, Mother. She didn't say it, though. Self-centered or not, her mom was obviously upset. "Look, I need to go. I have to get him out."

"Just a minute. Let me help. I'll call your father's lawyer, Saul Goldberg. He's the best. I'll even pay. It's the least I can do since it was all my fault."

Jordan softened at her mother's unusual tenderness. "Mom, how nice, but Eddie's innocent. He won't need a high-powered attorney like Saul."

"I really want to help. Are you sure?"

"Yes, I am." The tears had stopped. Since when did talking to Mary calm her down? A conversation with her overbearing, control freak mother usually ramped things up. Now *there* was something to think about later. She sniffed again. "I need to go blow my nose."

"Call me if you need me, dear. You know I'm always here for you."

Right, Mom. Here, there, and everywhere.

JORDAN'S NEXT MOVE WAS to call Ryan Avery, *her* choice of attorney, and notify him to set up a bail bond. Ryan was an ex-corporate attorney from New York. He knew what he was doing and didn't waste any time getting down to it.

Ryan was a man of his word.

Jordan was able to pick up Eddie in front of lockup at three thirty, only six hours later. He was a different man than the one who'd walked out the door in the morning. No defiance. No arrogance.

Somber.

She held him in her arms, trying to ignore the odd odor clinging to him. "You okay?"

"I'm good. Not like it's my first time in jail," he said quietly.

He put on a good act, but it was obvious that beneath the surface he was more than a little affected by the experience. Years ago, when Eddie worked for Cleveland crime lord Anthony Vercelli he probably had seen the inside of a cell. But he was done with the mob, had been for a while. She wanted to think he was a different man now—the kind lockup would get to.

"So, did I miss anything?"

"Nothing I can think of." She tossed him the keys. "You drive."

He cocked a brow. "Like I wasn't going to?"

There he was. She could breathe a little easier. This was the man she knew how to deal with. "Gina is going to sweet-talk our clients and see if we can get extensions on all the ongoing cases that aren't an emergency. That way we can dedicate ourselves to this one."

She opened the window and turned her head toward it to breathe. He didn't seem to notice.

Eddie pulled out into the downtown Phoenix traffic.

"So, did you think up a plan in the last few hours? I mean, since you had some time to kill?"

"Ha-ha," he said. "My plan is to shower, then we go to work. Lockup stinks. I need to wash it off."

"I wasn't going to say anything, but—"

He even laughed. "Yeah, but you rolled down the window."

"Okay," she said. "I'll leave you at your place, give you some time to get your head back in it while I check on things at the office. I'll pick you up later and we'll put a game plan together."

She didn't need to check on things at the agency. It was probably running better now than when she'd been in charge. Eddie's niece, Gina, was like a mini-drill sergeant when it came to keeping things in line. What Jordan really had to do was figure out how to run interference for the agency. It wouldn't look good once word got around one of its principals was arrested for murder and for stealing something they'd been hired to guard.

THE HOT SHOWER WAS like a baptism/rebirth/renewal. So much had happened since Thursday morning, when they discovered the crime scene. It was hard to believe it was only Friday afternoon.

Well, at least he didn't smell like winos and stale urine anymore. Eddie stepped out of the shower. Where the heck did he put his towel? The bathroom was so steamy, he couldn't even see himself in the mirror, much less—

"Hey, Eddie."

He whipped around, regretting he hadn't brought a weapon in with him. It could have turned out badly. Stupid. Off his game.

But this time it was only ... "What are you doing here, Sofia?"

The steam cleared, and there she was. Sofia Vercelli, the daughter of crime boss Anthony Vercelli and Eddie's old squeeze, leaned against the doorjamb. All five foot one of her. Her eyes swept him top to bottom and back up, pausing somewhere around the middle. Oh, yeah, naked. Not that it mattered. She'd seen him naked before, plenty of times.

She looked the same. Frickin' gorgeous. Her black hair was shorter and fuller than when they'd been together, but the rest of the package was just like he remembered. Petite, slim, stacked. Sultry as hell. *Don't even think about it, Marino. She's toxic.*

"You're lookin' good." She handed him the towel. "Been working out?"

He wrapped it around his waist. "What do you want?"

"Been missing you, baby."

"Look. I'm busy. How'd you get in, anyway?"

She pulled a gold chain from inside the low-cut sweater and waved a key at him. "You think I'd toss the key to your place, handsome? Not in a million years."

What the hell kind of security specialist am I? "Guess I forgot to change the locks, didn't I?"

He moved around her and went to the kitchen. Crap, wasn't this just what he needed today?

She scurried along behind him, her stilettos clicking on the hardwood floor like a puppy's nails. "I'm here to help you."

He snagged a bottle of water from the fridge, upended it, and drank it down. "Help me? How the hell can you help me?"

"I was all alone Wednesday night. Alone. That means nobody to talk to, nobody to see, nobody to say I wasn't with you." She purred like the sleek cat she was.

He waited. What was she talking about? Then it hit him. "You saying—?"

"I'm saying you're looking at your alibi. Right here." She put her hands on her hips, thrust out her ample breasts, and gave him those bedroom eyes. "Bet you never guessed."

What the hell was she up to? He knew her inside and out, literally. They'd been together a long time—until she'd deceived him. He would bet good money she had an ulterior motive.

Sofia wouldn't waste her time if there weren't something in it for her. "Alibi?" he asked. "How did you even know about the trouble I'm in?"

She shrugged. "Daddy. He's got a guy down at central lockup."

Daddy. Of course. She was Vercelli's daughter, all right. What would the old man say if he knew she was here, offering to lie for him, putting herself on the line? "Daddy won't appreciate you coming to my rescue."

Eddie was always careful to stay off Vercelli's bad side. They left things pretty dicey when they went their separate ways. Vercelli had wanted him to graduate from fixer to killer. Eddie wouldn't do it. He was one of the few people who left Vercelli's operation on two feet. Since then he'd been pretty much walking on eggshells around the powerful racketeer.

Sofia could complicate his fragile relationship with Anthony big time. *Why would she lie for me?* Why wouldn't she, was more like it. In the past she lied about him and *to* him. Why not for him?

"Something in it for you? You never do something for nothing."

She pouted. Funny how he used to think that was cute. "I was hoping it would put things in a better light—for us, I mean. Maybe you'd take a more favorable view of me."

"I'm with Jordan, now. There won't be any 'favorable view.' Not now. Not ever. Not even if you do this for me. You need to know that going in."

She smiled and moved close. "Yeah? We'll see." She slipped her arms around his neck. "I'm thinking you'll be grateful after I get you off the murder charges. Didn't you miss me, Eddie? Just a little?"

She raised her lips to his. He turned his head away.

"When I said I was giving you time to get your head back in the game, this wasn't what I had in mind."

Eddie looked over Sofia's head.

Jordan stood in the living room. If looks were daggers, he'd be stabbed through the heart.

Chapter 5

~

JORDAN WOULDN'T HAVE BEEN surprised if someone told her steam was coming out her ears.

Eddie backed away from the flashy girl, his face flush with guilt. His towel came loose and slipped off his hip, and he snatched it to cover himself.

Seriously? Isn't it a little late for that?

He was backpedaling as fast as he could, faster than she'd ever seen him do it before. "Jordan, it's not what it looks like."

"No? I really hope not, because it looks like you were standing in your kitchen, naked, kissing another woman."

He stuttered. "This is Sofia Vercelli."

The Sofia person waved manicured fingers in a casual greeting. Jordan resisted the urge to scratch her eyes out.

Wait a minute. Vercelli?

Jordan spit out, "Maybe you should get dressed while Sofia and I … chat."

"Yeah, right." He shook a finger at Jordan. "Play nice."

The Vercelli woman strutted into the living room and cocked an eyebrow while she watched Eddie head down the hallway. He flipped the towel around to cover his backside.

Jordan turned to Sofia. "Eddie have something in his eye?"

Sofia twisted her head. "No, why?"

"When I came in it looked like maybe you were trying to see if he had something in his eye."

Sofia smiled. "Very funny. Can I offer you something to drink?"

You? Offer me? Jordan ground her teeth and took a threatening step to tower over the shorter woman. There was occasionally something to be said for being five feet ten inches tall—the intimidation factor, for instance.

Sofia's quick intake of breath told Jordan her little bullying scheme had hit home. "What do you want with Eddie?"

"What does any woman want with Eddie?" Sofia's voice was low, throaty, and sexy, which made Jordan even angrier.

"I'm not going to play games with you," Jordan said.

"Oh, I get it. Eddie hasn't told you about us."

"Us? What do you mean us?" *Jealous much, Jordan?*

"Not so long ago Eddie was *my* man." Emphasis placed on *my*. "But he became too possessive," Sofia sighed, "and I had to break it off."

Eddie, possessive? He never seemed possessive to her. Not yet, anyway. She dug her nails into her palms and took a deep breath. "Look, Miss Vercelli. It's not a good time to mess with Eddie. He's facing serious charges."

"Charges? There won't be any charges. He's got an alibi. He was with me Wednesday night. All night." Sofia gave Jordan a sly look. "That ought to cover him. Don't you think?"

While Jordan picked her jaw up off the Norwegian hardwood, Sofia strutted out the door.

Jordan whipped around to face Eddie as he walked back into the room.

"What the hell, Marino? You were with her?"

He pushed his hands out defensively. "No, Jordan, if she said that …."

The doorbell rang. Eddie was literally saved by the bell,

but Jordan had no intention of letting it slide. They would be discussing this later, in depth.

TANK, DIEGO, EDDIE, AND Jordan all sat around his dining table drinking coffee, trying to come up with a plan of attack. There was so much to do, it boggled the mind: justice for Muggs, recover the Golden Dream coins, salvage the agency's reputation—all of which would get Eddie out of hot water. As difficult as it was, the matter of Sofia Vercelli would have to be sidelined, at least for a while.

Since neither Eddie nor Jordan seemed inclined to talk, Tank took charge of the meeting. Casting confused looks at them, he said, "All right, y'all. First things first. The knife. It is yours, right?"

"It is," Eddie said.

Diego rubbed his jaw. "Eddie, when did you last see that knife?"

"I don't know. It's been a while since I had it out of the bag. Months. Who keeps track of stuff like that?"

Diego was thoughtful. "Muggs was a fighter. How did they get the drop on him?"

Tank said, "There were no defensive wounds. Like he knew his killer."

Jordan put in her two cents. "I say we start with the Dahlonega coins. If we find them, we can trace them back to the killer."

"Makes sense," Tank agreed.

"You two guys," Eddie began, "check pawn shops, fences and black market dealers here, Tucson, L.A., Vegas, Nogales."

"Luis Martinez. He's my guy in Tucson, and he's taken risks on merchandise like this before." Diego stood and pulled out his cell.

"Merchandise like this?" Jordan asked. "You mean stolen?"

Diego nodded. "I'll put him on notice right now." He hit a button on his phone, put it against his ear then went to stand in front of the balcony door while he spoke in a low voice. When he came back to the table, he said, "I called my guys in Vegas, L.A., and Tucson. I'm emailing them what we have on the coin collection. They'll let me know if anything shows up."

"What else should we be doing?" Tank asked.

Eddie leaned back in his chair. "The minute we can, let's get Muggs's personal effects from the cops. Wallet, watch, and cellphone, all of it. Not likely, but maybe there'll be something we can use." He turned to Jordan. "Do you think Ann might let you into the museum before it reopens and everything gets wiped out?"

Jordan shrugged. "Maybe, as long as I make it clear you're not tagging along." She paused. "Has it occurred to you this isn't just about stealing the Golden Dream coins?"

He looked at her, waiting.

"Someone went to an awful lot of trouble to make it look like you pulled this off. Who would take such risks, go to such lengths?"

"A lot of people. I'm not all that popular."

"I was thinking about the job for the Brenners last year," Jordan said. "You know when Owen Shetland was killed. What about his people? What if his family or one of his men wanted revenge—against you?"

Eddie nodded. "Something to think about."

"Let's do more than think about it. We need to take a serious look at people connected to Shetland. I mean, why not?"

They had to get this handled, and fast.

Shea Investigations' reputation couldn't take a hit like five million dollars worth of gold coins disappearing on their watch.

Interruption came in the form of Eddie's nineteen-year-old niece, Gina, who swung open the door and came in.

They all turned and stared expectantly as she threw up her hands. The shake of her head tossed her ponytail. Her dark eyes, so much like Eddie's, were apologetic. "What is it you're always telling me, Uncle Eddie? Timing is everything."

From behind her, Eddie's mother, Rose, swept grandly into the room, arms open, voice shrill. "Eddie. Eddie, my boy."

Eddie stood. A look of disbelief crossed his face before he smiled. "Mama? What are you doing here?"

"Come here and give your mama a kiss."

He obeyed, bending down like the dutiful son Jordan knew him to be.

Rose beamed and pinched his cheek.

She turned and swept her intelligent eyes, the color of coffee beans, over Jordan. Seemingly satisfied, she held out her arms. Jordan walked into them and submitted to a proper squishing.

"I was worried about you, young lady," Rose said, referring, Jordan guessed, to the close encounter with the car bomb last year.

Gina gave Eddie the eye. "I told *Nonna* you were all here working hard, planning a big party."

Rose squealed in delight. "An engagement party, Eddie?"

Gina held up her hands. "Her idea, not mine."

"Mama Rose, we're not—" Jordan began.

Rose took Jordan's arm, pulled her next to Eddie and put their hands together. "I'm so happy. This could mean grandbabies. A little Eddie or Jordan."

The color drained from Eddie's face. *Serves him right, the louse.* Jordan crushed his hand and took pleasure in the effort he made not to wince. She made a quick sidestep to put a little distance between her and the object of her irritation while Rose continued, "You make such a beautiful couple. Aren't they such a beautiful couple, Mark?"

An older man wearing a red nylon jogging suit rolled into the room. The jacket was zipped up tight over his soft belly.

"Marky, sweetheart, come on over here and meet my Eddie. Eddie, this is Mark Garrity."

Eddie stood, lasering in with suspicious eyes on the stranger—not exactly a warm welcome.

The older gentleman didn't seem to notice. He offered his hand. "Glad to meet you, son. Heard so much about you."

"Funny, Marky," Eddie said, "I haven't heard anything about you." He glanced at his mother.

She gushed, "Marky and I are here to get your blessing, since you're the man of the family."

"Blessing?" Eddie swung back around to the older man.

Mark seemed oblivious to the coming storm. He smiled. Enormous teeth gleamed in his mouth, dominating his face. "I've asked my Rosie, my Sicilian flower, to marry me."

Thunder rolled over Eddie's face. Marky just grinned.

Ah, the bliss of the ignorant.

Chapter 6

⁓

Eddie left with Mama Rose and her boyfriend to head toward the hotel across the way where they were staying.

Jordan turned to Diego and Tank, who both stood stock still, their mouths hanging open.

"What?" she asked.

Tank's southern drawl was always slow but even more so now. "I just want to tell y'all how, uh, happy we are, you know, about you and Eddie, uh—"

"Oh," she said. "No. We're not. Not really."

It was hysterical how relieved they both looked. Jordan almost laughed.

Gina explained. "*Nonna* Rose has a knack for jumping to conclusions."

Jordan blinked. "Jumping to conclusions? Sounds like outright fiction to me."

Gina grinned. "Well, she is a writer, after all."

Rose's writing career was an irony in itself. At the age of sixty-five, she wrote and sold a gritty, sexy novella to *Pulp Crime* magazine. The issue in which it appeared sold a record number, and Mama Rose never looked back. Two years later, she was still going strong. Jordan always tried to be supportive and buy her work, but some of Rose's stories made her cringe. Her tough heroes and heroines wandered mean city streets solving murders born of greed and treachery. Yep, Mickey Spillane had nothing on Rose Marino.

Jordan changed the subject. "All right, Tank, Diego, you know the plan, right?" They nodded as she continued. "Let's get at it."

The men made quick work of leaving. She counted on those two, just as she always counted on Muggs. Inside something went queer, and her eyes stung for a moment. Eddie had to be struggling with the loss. It was an awkward time for Rose to show up, but in the end it might turn out to be serendipitous. Rose was a caring, nurturing person—unlike some mothers Jordan knew. The trick would be getting Eddie to come clean as to how he felt about his friend's death. When his father was killed, Gina had told her, the stoic young boy shouldered the responsibility of sheltering his mother from every storm. He'd been doing it ever since.

"Gina, can you lock up when you leave? Eddie said he wanted to take Rose out to dinner tonight. I ought to go along even though I'm mad as hell at him right now."

"You're mad at Eddie? How come?"

"For one thing, I guess I'm engaged, and I didn't even get a rock."

Gina laughed.

"For another, just exactly who is Sofia Vercelli? And, more importantly, who is she to Eddie?"

Gina's eyes opened wide, and she covered her mouth with her hand.

Jordan had the answer she needed. "That bad, eh? She was here earlier. Says Wednesday night she and Eddie were ...." She couldn't say it out loud. "Well, just lock up, Gina, okay? I'm going home to shower, change and make nice for Mama Rose tonight. We're about to hit the streets looking for Muggs's killer, and now here's your grandmother to deal with. I haven't the vaguest idea how to manage both."

Her hand was on the knob.

"Jordan?"

She turned and gave Gina her full attention. "Yes?"

"Eddie and Sofia? Ancient history."

"Hmm. I hope history isn't repeating itself."

DIEGO WAS FOLLOWING UP with his black market contacts, Tank was doing some checking on Owen Shetland's people, and she and Eddie were waiting to hear from Detective Ann Murphy as to whether the crime scene would be available to them. That meant there was no reason Jordan and Eddie shouldn't have dinner with Mama Rose and her beau, although it would be hard to keep up light chatter with their hearts so heavy.

Jordan chose a copper-colored wrap dress. She ignored the stilettos purchased specifically to wear with that dress and went with Tory Burch ballet flats so she and Mama Rose wouldn't look like Gandalf and Bilbo Baggins.

Eddie came by and picked her up.

She was ready and waiting at the front door. "Did you hear anything from Tank or Diego?"

"Nothing yet."

She sighed in frustration.

"Yeah," he said. "Tell me about it."

Investigations hardly ever went quickly, and waiting on this case might just push them both over the edge—Eddie more than Jordan.

They left in Jordan's Pilot since Eddie's Porsche wouldn't hold everyone. Eddie drove and swung by to pick up his mother and Mark.

Rose wore a Christmas-red Chanel suit and an odd little red hat over her frizzy salt-and-pepper hair.

She looked like a petite Italian tomato, and she positively

glowed. "Eddie, I'm so excited about you and Jordan."

"Me too, Mama." He looked sideways at Jordan.

She didn't bat an eyelash. *Go ahead, let's see you fast-talk your way out of this one.*

He sighed and turned his head slightly toward the backseat. "So, Mark, what's your gig?"

Mark cleared his throat. "I—"

Rose interrupted. "My Mark is a big-time movie producer."

Eddie looked as if he were trying to remember. "Have I ever heard of you?"

"I—"

Rose again. "Marky works abroad. You know, Eddie, like foreign films."

"Foreign films." Eddie's tone was drier than a good martini. "Perfect. Just perfect."

JORDAN'S BROTHER ALEC—THE BLUE-EYED spitting image of his handsome father, except with the golden brown hair of Ben's youth—looked impressively fit in his dark suit as he greeted them at the front entrance. The new Scottsdale location of Welsh's Steak and Chop House, owned by Jordan's mother and father, had opened three weeks earlier. Reservations were already hard to get. The local paper called it a winner, as impressive as the original near the Miracle Mile in Chicago.

Jordan had spent twenty minutes on the phone explaining to her mother that Eddie hadn't told Rose of his arrest, and it was a taboo subject. It was Mary's job to inform the rest of the family. Hopefully no one would bring it up.

"Welcome to Welsh's Steak and Chop House, Mrs. Marino. I'm Alec Welsh, Jordan's brother." Alec bent over Rose's hand and kissed it gallantly.

"How could I forget you, Alec? Oh, Jordan," Rose giggled, "your brother is such a hottie! I think he's even more handsome than when I met him at your mother's Christmas party." She turned flirtatious eyes to Alec. "We're going to be family, Alec. Call me Mama Rose."

"Family?" Alec gave Jordan an inquisitive look as he shook his head. "Older sister, maybe, but you're too young to call Mama."

Jordan smiled. Her older brother was such a class act.

Alec moved his wife Caroline and their twin girls out from Chicago to manage the new location. And so far, he'd done a stellar job. The oldest of the Welsh brood, he'd been chief protector and bodyguard to both Katie and Jordan while they were growing up.

Jordan would always be grateful for his support and compassion when she was studying at the Sorbonne and American University in Paris. Her lover Etienne had become controlling and possessive. Jordan was young, inexperienced, and had no real ammunition to defend herself. Eventually he grew tired of her, broke off their torrid relationship, and walked out. Jordan had never been in love before the older, arrogant Frenchman, and the break-up nearly killed her. Alec, attending the Cordon Bleu, was there for her, saved her. If not for him, she wouldn't have been the same after such a crushing experience. She loved her brother unconditionally.

For the Welsh's new restaurant, the remodel of an older building in central Scottsdale had turned out perfectly—classic steakhouse décor. White tablecloths, heavy straight-backed chairs, mahogany paneling. The open kitchen allowed customers to watch the well-trained staff hustle their chow. A slate-faced fireplace provided as much atmosphere as it did warmth to the back bar area. The clatter of dishes and low hum of conversation provided a cozy soundtrack. The aromas sold the menu even before patrons had a chance to look at it.

Alec led them to a circular table in the center of the restaurant. Ben and Mary Welsh sat waiting. From the extra empty glasses on the table, they'd been there a while.

Mary was fairly animated, and Jordan surmised she'd had

a couple. Mary confirmed by gushing, "Darling Rose, one of my favorite people. It's been way too long since we saw you at Christmas. You must make the trip from Cleveland more often."

Rose reached down and hugged Mary. "Don't get up, sweetie. I heard you have a bum ankle. How are you doing?"

"Oh, thanks so much for your kind words. It's been difficult." Mary laid a fluttering hand against her bosom. "I've been managing, though." She cut her eyes at the cane propped against the edge of the table.

Jordan mentally rolled her eyes, but made it a point not to actually do it.

Mary took Rose's hands. "I'm so delighted to see you again. You look so ..." Jordan caught her breath and sent a silent plea—*be nice, Mother,* "... festive."

Eddie leaned down and put his cheek beside Mary's. She took it like a trooper. Good.

Jordan released the breath. It might be an okay evening, although the jury was still out on whether she'd forgive Eddie. There would be time after dinner to bring up the subject of Sofia Vercelli, and Jordan had no intention of letting the occasion slide.

AFTER THE STEAKS—TOP QUALITY and done to perfection—Rose turned to Mary. "Have the kids set the date yet?"

"The date? What date?" Mary pursed her lips.

"What date?" Rose smiled. "The wedding, of course."

Mary nearly choked. "Jordan?"

Jordan looked at Eddie, who turned an odd shade of green.

"No." Jordan hurried to avert the tempest. "We're planning a long engagement."

Eddie added, "Yeah, like decades."

"Oh, Eddie, you're such a tease." Jordan kicked him under the table, hard.

Mary stood so quickly she nearly knocked over her chair,

the ankle obviously forgotten for the moment. "Oh, my God, wedding?"

Jordan stood and took Mary by the hand. "Mother, weren't you going to show me the new wine cellar?"

Mary stared at her. "Wine cellar?"

Jordan yanked. "Come on."

Apparently dumbstruck, Mary grabbed the cane and followed, barely favoring the "difficult" injured ankle. *Milk it much, Mom?* When they were a good distance from the table, she dug in her heels. "Jordan, something you'd like to tell your mother?"

Jordan quickly explained how Rose and Mark had come to Scottsdale to let Eddie know of their own wedding plans, how she'd come to believe Jordan and Eddie were engaged, and how Eddie had been reluctant to dispel the fantasy.

Jordan looked down into Mary's hazel eyes, so like her own. One of the things she always wondered about but would never have the nerve to ask was if her mother resented having a daughter four inches taller than she. "He'll tell her, Mother, when the time's right. Hearing about Muggs will be hard on her. Eddie says she used to cook special meatballs for 'all her boys' every Sunday afternoon."

"I see." Mary nodded slowly. "My lips are sealed. Eddie's mother is a sweet woman. I wouldn't want to hurt her. But I'm so relieved you're not marrying him. He's just not, well … you know."

Yes. She knew too well how conflicted her mother was when it came to Eddie Marino. She liked Eddie, thought he was a 'nice young man,' and spoke often of his many admirable traits. But she made it clear none of those traits made him a suitable candidate for son-in-law. It was a good thing she knew nothing of his history in organized crime. Jordan herself was conflicted about that.

Jordan sighed. "I don't think you have to worry about nuptials anytime soon. He's sort of on my bad side right now."

It was obvious from the concern on Mary's face that she had something more on her mind. "I'm going to say something to you. It may make you angry, but I'm compelled to tell it to you straight all the same. Someone from your agency has died on the job. It could have been you, Jordan."

Oh, man, here we go.

Mary took a deep breath and went on, "I'm begging you. If my ankle weren't shredded, I'd get down on my knees in supplication. Leave the agency. Sell your half to Eddie. Give it to him. Anything. Just leave. You were nearly blown to smithereens last year yet you ignored my pleas then. I'm asking you again. I couldn't bear it if anything happened to you. What if it were you on duty Wednesday night? That poor young man who died—?"

Jordan couldn't help herself. "Murdered, Mom. Muggs was murdered. Slaughtered."

Mary looked into Jordan's eyes. Her expression was sad, yet calm. None of the normal hysterics that usually accompanied Mary's demands for Jordan to give up her career were present tonight. It was as if she knew her plea would fall on deaf ears, but the urge to make her case was too strong. She'd already said as much. "You make my point for me."

Jordan gathered her mother in her arms. Mary didn't resist. "I love you, Mother. And even as different as you and I are, I understand where you're coming from. But I won't be leaving the agency, and I will be helping Eddie go after the killer."

She couldn't see Mary's face but felt the slight shudder rippling through her mother. "I know, Jordie. I know." Mary pulled back and avoided Jordan's eyes while she put a hand to her hair. "I won't say anything to Rose."

Jordan kissed Mary's cheek. Her mother seldom showed any empathy. When she did, it was touching.

Mary took another couple of minutes to fluff her dyed-to-match-Jordan's deep auburn hair before they returned to the table, where coffee and several gorgeous desserts had been served. Eddie stood and held Mary's chair as she sat and laid her hand on Rose's. "I hear you and Mark have pending nuptials of your own."

Rose beamed and nodded, her mouth occupied with the kitchen's famous tiramisu.

Mary went on. "I insist on throwing the two of you an engagement party at my home. Let's say next Friday. Impromptu as it is, I'm sure we'll still have all the right people there."

"An engagement party?" Rose looked pleased.

Eddie looked panicked. "Isn't that a little premature?"

"Nonsense." Mary waved him away.

Jordan sat back and slid a spoonful of *crème brûlée* into her mouth. If the circumstances of the murder and robbery hadn't been so dire, the Eddie, Mary, and Rose show might be fun.

"Friday?" Mark laid his hand atop Rose's. "Sweetheart, when's your meeting with the studio? Don't want to cause any problems with your big deal now, do we?"

Eddie looked at his mother. "Studio?"

"Oh, I forgot to mention it. I just sold the rights to my serial killer story. They're going to make a movie out of it."

Eddie folded his arms. "It's not a foreign film, is it?"

"No. Marky isn't producing. Not yet, anyway. Maybe later on."

"What did you score on this deal, Mama?" Eddie's eyes narrowed on Mark.

Mark smiled. All those white teeth gleamed. "Two hundred large."

Even Mary seemed impressed. "Two hundred thousand dollars?"

Rose demurred. "That's only if I write the screenplay."

Mark seemed to have no doubt. "Oh, she'll write it."

Eddie turned to his mother. "You forgot to mention two hundred thousand dollars?" He lifted his glass. "*Cent'anni*, Mama." Something else seemed to occur to him. "When exactly did you and Mark …" he had trouble spitting it out, "… get, um, together?"

"It was so funny. I was having breakfast at the IHOP—you know I love those blueberry pancakes—and up walks this gorgeous man." Her adoring gaze rested on Mark. "He recognized me from my picture in the newspaper article about my big break."

"Oh, he *recognized* you, did he?" He glared at Mark.

"Mm-hmm, and we just hit it off."

Was Eddie grinding his teeth? "I'll just bet you did."

Chapter 7

～

IT WAS AFTER TEN Friday night when Eddie drove Jordan home and walked her to the door.

"Good night," she said. It had been a long, exhausting day, and all she wanted to do was go to bed.

He reached up and laid his hand against the open door. "Just wait a minute, Jordan. We can't leave things like this. You know they say, 'Never go to bed angry.'"

"I'm not angry. Not really." She turned away, and he followed her inside.

The image of Eddie with Sofia Vercelli was imprinted on her brain. But she had it in mind to put it aside until Eddie was in better shape. Piling more stress on top of all he was already dealing with would not only be cruel and insensitive, it would also be stupid. He was much better at a good rousing argument than she. Better to wait until things had settled down to bring up the subject—but it was definitely a matter she intended to learn more about.

Jordan made her way through the house, opened the patio door, and followed Sadie outside. She stood by the pool staring at the half-moon mirrored in the inky water. Jordan shivered in the cool breeze that rippled the reflection. March days in Scottsdale were perfect—warm, in the upper seventies, low eighties. But the evenings cooled down to the low fifties. The desert air was clean, seasoned with the faint scent of mesquite, creosote, and the chlorine in the pool.

She rubbed her bare arms. Eddie moved up behind her, slipped off his jacket and draped it around her shoulders.

He put his arms around her. "You know I wasn't with her that night."

"Why would she say it if it wasn't true?"

"I'm pretty sure she figures if she does this I might take her back."

Jordan looked up, trying to see his face, but it was cloaked in darkness.

"It's never going to happen. I told her I'm with you now. While I don't want anything to do with her, if her story gets me off the hook, I'll run with it. I can't revenge Muggs if I'm sitting in a jail cell."

"You think I don't know that?" Jordan said. "She's willing to lie for you? To the cops? She must want you back real bad."

Eddie moved his hands to her shoulders and turned her around. "It's all one-sided. Don't pretend you don't know that." He pulled her close and kissed her hard, long, and smoking hot as Louisiana pepper sauce. It burned all the way to her toes.

Eddie, the man she was born to love. She threw herself into the kiss, and before she really knew what was happening, they'd made their way into the house and were pulling at each other's clothes.

He took hold of one of her legs behind the knee and lifted it. She wrapped it around him as he reached under the dress and caught the edge of her panties with the curl of a finger.

Within seconds the panties were tossed to the side. While he shrugged out of his shirt, she unzipped his pants.

"You have one?" she whispered.

She wasn't sure where it came from, but he produced a

condom. She took it from him, and looking straight into his eyes, ripped the wrapper with her teeth, snapped it open, and slipped it on him.

The low sound he made in his throat drove her crazy.

"Jesus, Jordan," he growled.

That did it. A thrill shot through Jordan, and she was done.

She laid her hands against his chest and pushed him down onto the sofa. Together they pulled her dress off over her head. She straddled him and lowered herself onto him, catching her breath as he filled her.

Moments later they lay exhausted, contemplating the detonation that went off between them. Sadie padded in through the open patio door and licked Jordan's hand.

"One for the history books." Eddie was out of breath. "Where the hell did that come from?"

Jordan didn't say it out loud, but she was pretty sure they had Sofia Vercelli to thank for what just happened between them.

THE RINGING OF EDDIE's cellphone woke Jordan. He lay on his side propped on his elbow, looking down at her. "Sorry, babe. It's Ann Murphy. I better take it." He sat up. "Hello?"

Jordan stretched and looked at the clock—almost nine forty-five Saturday morning. Their lie-in was courtesy of the marathon sex they'd indulged in all through the night.

"Uh-huh. Uh-huh. Sure. Right." Eddie and Ann seemed to be having a one-sided conversation with Ann doing all the talking.

"Yeah? What a relief." Eddie cut his eyes at her and swiped a hand across his brow.

"Okay. Thanks for letting me know." He paused, then, "Say, I don't suppose you could do me one large and light a fire under the ME? It would mean a lot. Muggs's parents are hurting. They need to lay their son to rest, and his dad's in pretty bad shape."

Jordan got up and let Sadie out. When she crawled back between the sheets wearing nothing but her Victoria's Secret

Man-killer Special, he rolled up beside her. For a minute, she thought the morning would be a replay of the night before, but instead he kissed her soundly and threw back the sheets.

"Well, Sofia did it." He absently caressed her breasts, perkier-than-normal courtesy of the hi-tech bra. "She went down to the Scottsdale PD and made a statement providing an alibi."

He went on. "I'm no longer a suspect, at least as far as Ann Murphy's concerned. She believes someone's trying to set me up. But she says good old Detective Thompson has a hard-on for me. Says he's like a dog after a T-bone to pin this on me and has plans to use the evidence he snagged out of my car to build a case. Ann's trying to keep a leash on him, but I don't know how long that'll last. She didn't say it in so many words, but I could tell she was pissed off about the Sofia thing. She thinks I was cheating on you."

"If Ann's going to buy the alibi, she has to think the worst of you. And good old Detective Thompson never was a member of your fan club. What is it about you that police can't stand?"

"Gotta be my animal magnetism." He lifted his hand to caress her face. "I'm sorry she has to think that of me, at least for now. But to tell the truth, I only really care what you believe."

Jordan looked into his eyes. "I'm trying," she said. "It's hard."

He went into the bathroom and turned on Jordan's awesome steam shower.

Jordan tossed off the covers, hopped up and went to make coffee. By the time Eddie walked in twenty minutes later, he was buttoning his shirt.

He moved her hair aside and dropped a kiss on the back of her neck. "Since I'm in the clear, at least with Ann, she's made arrangements for me to get into the museum and have a look around. I'm going to my place for a change of clothes, meet Mama for coffee then head on down there. You coming?"

Chapter 8

~

AFTER A STOP AT Eddie's place, they met Rose and Mark at the hotel coffee shop for brunch. The place was slow for a Saturday morning during Spring Break, then again, not many college students could afford the five-star resort Mama Rose and Mark had booked.

Eddie's mother and her intended were dressed alike in matching purple golf shirts and khaki walking shorts. There was something so sweet about it Eddie didn't even pretend to find it annoying.

Mother Mary, please let him be on the level. Mama deserves some happiness.

He fidgeted through the Belgian waffles, coffee, and chitchat then finally took Rose's hand. "Let's go for a little stroll outside, Mama."

She gave him an odd look but went with him just outside to a brick-paved courtyard shaded by mid-size bushy palms in huge Mexican clay pots. He guided her to a cast-concrete bench that might have been made for a formal Italian garden.

She sat down and looked around. "It's beautiful out here."

When he didn't answer, she asked, "What is it, Eddie? Tell me and get it over with."

He sat beside her, took her hands between his, and told her what had happened to Muggs.

She wept. He held her. When she stopped crying, he wept, and she held him. He couldn't bring himself to speak of his arrest. This was her time, and they'd straighten the rest out eventually.

After a while, she stood, pulled her shorts up and her golf shirt down. "We're gonna miss that boy every day."

Hand in hand, they returned to the coffee shop where Mark and Jordan waited.

IT WAS A LITTLE after noon when Eddie and Jordan headed south on Scottsdale Road to the historic Wild West ambiance of Old Town Scottsdale and the Arizona Heritage Museum. Eddie put down the ragtop, and Jordan pulled her hair up in a scrunchie. The weather was so beautiful it nearly broke her heart. Azure sky. No clouds. Cool breeze. And, and, *ah-ah-choo*! Pollen everywhere. But the warm sun on her face was worth it. Almost.

Eddie was quiet until Jordan asked, "Did Ann say whether they got anything good from the crime scene?"

"Said they couldn't pull a single print."

"But the creeps messed with the alarm and the video systems. Right? With your expertise we might get a leg up."

He turned west onto Fifth Avenue. "That's what I'm hoping."

"And the point of entry?"

"The back door. They can't figure out why Muggs was killed in the exhibit room, not at the back entrance."

It hurt to talk about it. "They didn't have to kill him."

"Someone was out for blood." With the air whipping past, she barely made out what he said.

"It seems like they had a good plan," she said. "Smart guys."

"Not so smart we won't catch up with them." Steel in his voice.

EDDIE TOOK HIS GLOCK from the glove box, tucked it into the back of his jeans, and pulled his shirt down over it. The museum's front door was unlocked. The place was obviously still considered a crime scene, as confirmed by the heavy-handed use of yellow tape, but there was no sign of the cop Ann had said would be on duty to let them in.

They walked in unchecked.

"Let's head to the utility room first. The alarm set-up is a beaut. It's back there, and we can check out how these guys got around it and through the door." He walked faster. Jordan's long legs easily matched his stride.

Eddie seemed to be thinking along the same lines as she—to get a move on and take full advantage of the chance to wander around unsupervised.

They made their way around the front desk, by unspoken agreement skirting the room where the theft occurred—and Muggs was killed.

As they approached the back room, a mechanical clank came from the opposite end of the building. They stopped dead in their tracks.

"What was that?" she whispered.

"Somebody's here," Eddie whispered back and pulled his Glock as he gently moved Jordan behind him.

They turned around and crept toward an open door at the far side of the museum. Maybe the duty officer was back there after all. But according to Ann, the museum was closed and empty. If that was the case, why was fluorescent light streaming from the room?

Eddie moved up beside the door then turned inside, gun leveled. Jordan moved in behind him and looked over his shoulder.

Well, it definitely wasn't the duty officer.

A smallish man was crouched half-in, half-out of the lower portion of a credenza against the wall on the far side of what looked to be an administrative office.

He mumbled and swore softly.

The view included a good portion of pale backside and plumber's crack exposed by his drooping trousers.

"Gotcha," Eddie warned. "Go ahead, make a move. I'm dying to shoot you."

The man pulled back so fast his head slammed into the top of the open cabinet. "Damn."

Eddie took way too much pleasure in drawing down on him.

Jordan laid her hand on Eddie's arm. "Hold on there, Quick Draw. It's Mr. Hunter, the curator."

Hunter got to his feet and rubbed his head. "That's gonna make a lump."

"What are you doing here?" Eddie holstered the gun.

"I work here, son. What about you?" He recognized Jordan. "Oh, Miss Welsh. Shea Security. Right?"

"Mr. Hunter, this is my partner, Eddie Marino."

Eddie shook Hunter's hand. "Sorry about the gun. We expected an officer to be here to let us in."

"Sent him out for coffee. I'm pretty frustrated. Been trying to print the list of stolen items for the PD, but the stupid printer's broken. I just can't seem to get it fixed."

Eddie nodded and smiled. His expression was smug, his condescending attitude on full display. He tended to forget that everyone on the planet wasn't as tech savvy as he.

He walked—no, sauntered—across the room, took hold of the power cord and plugged it into a socket. "Try it now."

The older man shrugged and grinned sheepishly. "Well, whaddya know?"

"Since I've made it possible for you to print this, can we get a copy?"

Another shrug. "Don't see why not."

THE ALARM SYSTEM CONTROL board and keypad were housed in the utility room by the rear entrance. Stacks of supplies, a couple of mid-sized flatbed trolleys, two upright dollies, and several crates and boxes took up most of the space. Altogether it was a pretty tight squeeze with the two of them in there.

First they had a look at the jimmied lock. She leaned in over him, inhaling his essence—soap, shampoo, and Aramis cologne. She called it *Eau de Eddie.*

"Nice job, fairly clean," Eddie said, "but not necessarily the work of a specialist." He bent down for a look at the crossbar on the floor. One end of it was ragged and discolored. "Blow torch," he said. "I'd bet on it."

"Me, too. And my money rides with you. No prints on the keypad?"

"Not according to Ann. She said they dusted every-damn-where." He opened the control panel to the alarm and security system.

She backed off and gave him space, just letting him do his thing. Nobody was as good as Eddie when it came to electronics and security. To Jordan it resembled the control panel of a 747 jetliner. Even before the incident, she had known it was a real whiz bang of a system. Or so Eddie had told her.

Eddie said, "Really nice set-up, isn't it? They spent *mucho dinero* here. Sophisticated stuff."

"Yeah?"

"And see that?" He pointed to two places inside the panel box where tiny clips had been placed over circuits. "That's good news for us."

"How's that?"

"Getting in the door? Nothing special. Anyone can bust a lock and melt down a crossbar. B and E 101. But disabling this complicated sweetheart of a system takes finesse and expertise. If they made a mess of things it would be different. In that case, we could be looking at hundreds of thieves, but I can only think of two, maybe three guys in the whole valley whose work is this pristine, who could disable a system this complex without setting off bells and whistles all over town."

If Eddie's list of possible specialists was short, the path to catching Muggs's killer might not be as long as they first thought.

"Could make our job a whole lot easier," Jordan said. "I'll call the Abromowitz girls. They'll be glad to hear we're making at least some progress."

Chapter 9

~

ARLY MONDAY MORNING JORDAN went straight to Eddie's
office. He had spent the majority of his Sunday reviewing
video surveillance tapes from the Arizona Heritage Museum,
looking for familiar faces. She'd rather not think about the fact
that he knew most of the local thieves from his days with the
Vercelli crime organization.

"Did you find anything on the tapes?" she asked.

He shook his head. "I went back weeks. Never saw anyone
who looked even vaguely familiar, and when they disarmed
the alarm system, they also disabled the video watchdog. There
won't be any help from there."

Gina came in and laid a stack of mail on the corner of his
desk.

Before she turned away, he said, "Hang on a minute." Eddie
closed his laptop and folded his long-fingered hands on top.

Gina stopped and turned expectantly.

"Can you to do something for me, Gina? Mama can't know
about it."

That got Jordan's attention, and apparently Gina's too. "A
secret. Awesome. I love a good secret."

And from what Jordan knew of her, she could keep one.

"I'd like you to check into this Marky—Mark Garrity guy," Eddie said. "Something's just—I don't know—*off* about this character."

"What do you want to know about him?" Gina's voice was hushed with excitement.

Eddie's was steady and deliberate. "Everything. Shoe size. Briefs or boxers. Does he have a current prescription for Viagra? I want to know everything."

TANK WALTZED IN AROUND ten. He'd called earlier to say that even though the Arizona Heritage Museum case was an ongoing investigation, a lady friend of his who manned the evidence room gave him access to everything the cops had in exchange for an overnight romp in the sack.

Tank went straight to Eddie's office. While there were bags under his eyes and he complained of an aching back, he still sported a cocky grin.

Jordan teased, "Not much sleep last night, huh, Tank?"

"I been workin' long, hard hours, ma'am, and I got something real good to show y'all."

He pulled a cellphone from his pocket and laid it on the desk. "My little gal down at PD headquarters was a big help."

Eddie smirked. "I just bet she was."

"Boss, you know us Southern boys don't kiss and tell. This here is Muggs's cell phone. They hadn't logged it in yet. I also snapped pictures of everything in his wallet."

"Tank, you rock." Jordan leaned over and kissed him on the cheek. He blushed and shuffled his feet.

Eddie picked up the phone. "You don't mind if I just say thanks and forgo the kissing, do you?"

"You know, boss, we're at least a couple of steps ahead of the cops. Chastity says they haven't been able to crack his password. If anything's on his phone, they don't have it yet."

Eddie looked up at him and grinned. "Chastity, eh? Let's not tell her I happen to know Muggs's password is 'Big Lebowski.' He loved that movie, knew it by heart."

It only took a couple of minutes for Eddie to gain access to the phone and find something so significant he pushed back from his desk, stood and began to pace. "This could be it, you guys. This could blow the case wide open for us."

He spun to face them and slid his fingers over the phone screen to enlarge one of the photos. "Get a load of this."

Jordan and Tank leaned close. It was a grainy close-up of a man's blood-smeared wrist. Peeking from under a black sleeve was a partial tattoo.

"What are we looking at?" Jordan twisted her head for a better view.

Eddie's voice took on that honeyed tone. Her knees turned to pudding whenever he used it. "Sweetcakes, you saying you don't know a prison tattoo when you see one?"

She caught her breath. Their eyes met. "This is big, Eddie."

Mama Rose's voice carried from the front room. "Oh, my gawd! I know who did it."

Eddie collapsed onto his sofa. "Aw, here it comes."

Resplendent in a hot pink jogging suit, Rose whooshed in like the Tasmanian Devil. "Eddie, Eddie! I solved the case."

Jordan fought to keep from laughing. Really? *Good. Case solved? Let's just take the rest of the day off then.*

Tank turned to leave the room. "Y'all need me, just let me know."

"Coward." Eddie got up and handed the phone to Tank. "Ask Diego to see what he can find out about the, uh, picture we were looking at. Will ya?"

"Oh, right. No problem, boss."

Seemed like Mama Rose was all wound up. "Didn't you hear me?" She practically shrieked. "I solved the case!"

Eddie guided her to the sofa and sat beside her. "Okay, Mama. Who was it?"

She popped back up, nodding in excitement. "The mob."

"The mob?" Jordan asked.

"Ya think?" Eddie rubbed his eyes.

Rose looked from Eddie to Jordan and sat down, deflated. "I don't understand. I thought you'd be happy."

Eddie smiled gently. "We are happy, Mama. Why don't you tell us why you think it's the mob?"

Rose squared her shoulders and sat up straighter. "Okay. So you remember like in *Goodfellas* how organized they were with the Lufthansa heist?"

Jordan shook her head.

"Better refresh our memories on this one, Mama," Eddie said, not unkindly.

"It really happened." Mama Rose warmed up. "Nineteen seventy-eight at JFK. It was a big job, you see, over eight million in cash and jewelry stolen. No small potatoes back then."

Jordan whistled. *No small potatoes now.*

Mama Rose went on. "It was an inside job. The mob guys had help from some goomba working at the airport. It's very famous."

"Okay, and …?" Jordan coaxed her.

"They did the smart thing and laid low after, at least in the movie. Never spent a nickel of the loot until one bozo screwed the pooch, bought his wife a new Cadillac. Stupid goomba got his comeuppance from the mob boss."

"Right." Eddie's legendary impatience reared its head. "So how does that tie in here?"

But Jordan and Mama Rose were on the same page. "Brilliant, Mama Rose."

Eddie cocked an eyebrow. "It is?"

"Sure. It makes perfect sense." Jordan spread her hands.

"It does?" Eddie again.

Rose patted Eddie's hand. "Catch up, son."

"Maybe you should spell it out for him, Mama Rose."

Rose shrugged. "None of the coins from the Arizona museum have turned up, right?"

"Just the ones they planted in my car," Eddie said, "And …?"

"Your ordinary crook would run to the nearest pawnshop. The mob? They know the score, know they gotta lay low until the heat's off, then just take their sweet time unloading the goods to the highest bidder."

A light bulb seemed to click on over Eddie's head. He looked at Jordan. She smiled and raised an eyebrow.

The old girl was good.

Diego stuck his head in the door. "We caught a break. Guess what just turned up?"

Jordan, Eddie, and Rose all looked at Diego.

Diego milked it. "In Tucson? Like magic?"

"Spit it out," Eddie said.

"My guy in Tucson is pretty sure he's got one of the Dahlonega coins. Said it was brought in for appraisal as a teaser for a, get this, much larger collection."

"Who brought it in?" Jordan asked.

Diego shrugged. "My guy didn't know him, but he's willing to hang on to the coin so we can have a look at it."

Eddie turned to Jordan. "You don't need to mention this to your BFF, Detective Murphy."

Jordan frowned. "Gee, Eddie. Good thing you reminded me. I had it in my head to go running straight down to tell her."

He blew out a puff of air. "Smart ass."

"Look who's talking," she snapped back.

Rose sighed. "This reminds me of the good old days with Eddie's father. Nothing like make-up sex after a rousing good fight."

Eddie looked at Rose in horror.

Jordan held back the laughter. She tried but couldn't stop the grin that spread across her face. "That's awesome news, Diego. One of the coins turned up!" Jordan congratulated him.

Mama Rose looked depressed. "There goes my theory about the mob keeping them under wraps." She sighed. "Shot all to hell."

Eddie patted her shoulder. "It's okay, Mama. It was a good theory."

Chapter 10

⁓

JORDAN AND EDDIE LEFT Scottsdale around noon on Monday and took I-10 southeast to Tucson.

Lucky Louie's Pawn Shop on South Fourth Avenue in South Tucson was a stand-alone white stucco building with security cameras all around and iron bars on the windows and doors. Jordan had only been to Tucson a few times and never in this part of town. All the gorgeous resorts and eclectic shops were north, nearer the Catalina Mountains. The area was definitely the kind of place where the term *armed and dangerous* referred to a majority of the general population.

Jordan took a lesson from Eddie, who wore ragged jeans, biker boots, and a couple of T-shirts layered over each other under a faded zip-up hoodie. She went with old jeans, a plain Army drab T-shirt and a black hoodie. The idea was to blend in with the neighborhood and avoid having to even think about problems with the locals—problems like getting mugged.

At Lucky's front door, a bald Latino with a handlebar moustache and muscles in spades intercepted them. "Dude, you packing?"

Eddie nodded and submitted to a thorough pat down.

When the big man moved to relieve Eddie of the Glock, Eddie grabbed his arm. "Uh-uh. That stays with me."

"Then you won't be going inside today, holmes."

"Luis is expecting us," Eddie said. "Eddie Marino."

"Wait outside."

Within a couple of minutes, the big guard came back and led them around the building to a rear door. It and the wrought-iron security gate were unlocked from the inside, and Eddie and Jordan were ushered into a square room measuring about twelve by twelve. Boxes and various cases were stored on gorilla shelves along the walls. In the center of the room, an old wooden table hosted two freestanding true-color lamps, several jeweler's loupes, and piles of merchandise items such as jewelry, guns, and small electronic devices. An enormous old-fashioned safe stood in one corner.

"*Señor* Marino?" A short Mexican man with a full head of wavy black hair and a body like a beach ball shook hands with Eddie. He sported what had to be two full carats in each ear and at least three pounds of gold bling around his neck. "Your reputation precedes you, *amigo*. I've heard many things about you and your powerful employer. I'm Luis Martinez, Lucky Louie to my homies." Martinez spoke perfect English with the elongated vowels and staccato consonants of someone born in Mexico.

Eddie said, "I don't work for the powerful man anymore, but we're still connected."

Martinez motioned toward a filthy loveseat on the far side of the room.

Jordan shook her head.

"We're good. Thanks," Eddie said.

Luis crossed to the safe, covered the dial with his body and spent a minute fiddling with it. Once it was open, he removed a small metal box, carried it to the table, switched on one of the lights and removed a clear acrylic case surrounding an uneven, rough-hewn gold coin.

"My friend Diego tells me you have an interest in this."

Jordan tried to be cool but wasn't sure she pulled it off. She could hear her own rapid, shallow breathing. She hoped her heart wasn't pounding as loud as it seemed to be.

Eddie reached out then stopped. "May I?"

Luis moved back a step and nodded.

Eddie sat in the chair at the table, picked up a loupe and examined the coin under the light.

He looked up at Jordan with a grim smile. "It's a Type One Dahlonega gold dollar."

She caught her breath. Something fluttered in her chest. She wasn't ashamed to acknowledge her excitement at the thought this could be the beginning of the end for Muggs's killer.

Eddie looked up at Lucky Louie. "This is one of them. What do you know about it?"

Luis shrugged. "Just what I told Diego. It was brought in by someone I've done business with for appraisal and to show as a sample to people I know in Mexico who might be interested in acquiring an entire collection."

"When's he coming back?"

Again, Luis shrugged. "When I tell him I have a buyer. I explained this is not something you just put on eBay."

Jordan laughed, but felt stupid when both Eddie and Luis looked at her. To redeem herself, she asked, "Do you have security footage of the guy?"

"*Sí*, of course. Everyone gets his picture taken. When we go to the front, you will too, *chica*." He winked.

He put the coin back in the safe, spun the dial, and led them to the front section of the store and into a small office area where remote security monitors were set up. Jordan glanced around at each one, quickly looking back down when Luis laughed and said, "Smile for the camera."

He went straight to the monitor, scrolled back a ways then fast-forwarded, and froze the picture. A lean young Latino stood at the counter. He wore a leather jacket that looked like it might have set him back six or eight hundred bucks and a diamond ring so big Jordan was surprised he could lift his hand.

"Do you recognize him?" she asked.

Eddie shook his head. "Lucky, think we can get a print?"

"No problem, *amigo*."

"And now I'm going to ask you to do something you're not going to like." Eddie turned serious eyes to Luis. "I want you to set him up for us. It'll mean the sale. You'll lose your commission—"

"I look that stupid to you?"

Eddie pressed. "Of course not. You look really smart to me, like someone smart enough to know I'm the go-to guy when you need a big favor. Like you said, I have powerful friends."

Jordan hated it when Eddie talked like that. It chilled her to the bone. Ninety-nine days out of one hundred, she'd bet her bottom dollar he was done with Vercelli and the dark life he'd led years ago. On days like this, when he made it sound as if he were still connected, she couldn't help but wonder.

Luis obviously believed Eddie could still get things done. He reached out and shook his hand. "*Es bueno*, Marino. A favor from your friends is worth ten times the commission I'd get on this sale."

Chapter 11

JORDAN MET ANN MURPHY just after eight Tuesday morning at a downtown coffee shop on Scottsdale Road near the PD headquarters. Ann was waiting when she got there, nursing a bottle of OJ.

"Morning, Miss Jordan."

"Morning, Detective Murphy." They hugged. "How's married life treating you?" *Better get the skinny on this marriage stuff. If Mama Rose has her way, I'll be joining those ranks sooner rather than later.*

Jordan set her coffee on the table and sat down.

"What's with the OJ? You pregnant?" Jordan asked.

Ann ran her hands over her belly. "Do I look like I'm putting on weight?

"No," Jordan laughed. "I'm just teasing you."

"Whew," Ann swiped her brow. "Okay. So the ME's report," her voice dropped, "on your friend Marvin—"

"Muggs. We called him Muggs." Jordan clenched her fists against the sudden sadness rolling over her. "What can you tell me?"

"Cause of death, stab wounds to the right upper quadrant.

He died of a pneumothorax and hemorrhagic shock."

Jordan's throat constricted. "He suffered." She choked, fighting back the tears.

"Sorry. I know it's hard to hear." Ann waited quietly while Jordan got herself together.

"These reports sound like a garage mechanic checking out a car. Why is the ME always so clinical? Muggs was so full of life. We miss him." Her throat tightened, and her belly ached. *Muggs*. "Look, Annie, I'm gonna go."

As she stood, Ann reached up and laid her hand on Jordan's arm. "Stay a minute. Something I have to tell you. You know Eddie was cleared?"

Jordan nodded.

Ann wouldn't look her in the eye. She stuttered and wrung her hands. "The alibi that cleared him. It was a … a …."

"Another woman." Jordan let her friend off the hook. "Eddie told me."

Ann looked relieved. "I didn't know how to tell you, but I knew I had to. I always have your back."

Jordan squeezed Ann's hand. "You're a good friend. Thanks."

"So how are things, between you and Eddie I mean?

The truth came easily in this case. "We're dealing with it."

"Good," Ann said, "because if you weren't, I was hoping you'd let me shoot him for you."

ONCE EDDIE GOT THE news the body was about to be released, he called Muggs's parents and told them. Muggs had been a man at ease with his own mortality and had told Eddie his idea of a perfect sendoff. Eddie paid for the cremation and had the ashes shipped to Muggs's family in Cleveland. With their permission he kept some of the ashes with him. He made it clear the last goodbye would be the way Muggs wanted it.

"The old man's taking it real hard," Eddie said, unable to look away from the small container of ashes on his office shelf. "Like he doesn't have enough to deal with. Said he never figured to outlive his son, for the love of God. Muggs's mom is worried all this stress might do him in."

Eddie's concern for Mr. and Mrs. Baxter touched Jordan. Beneath that hard edge he was tenderhearted.

Diego called and asked Eddie to meet him downtown at a certain deli near the Fourth Avenue Jail.

"Diego's got his hands on Owen Shetland's brother. I'm going down there."

"Wait up, Marino." Jordan hurried to her desk and removed her gun—a Smith & Wesson 38 six-shooter. It was so substantial that when she first started carrying it, she had to do wrist exercises. She slipped it in the exterior pocket of her bag—a gorgeous Maraschino cherry-red leather cross-body chosen specifically for easy-access to anything in the zippered compartment.

He gave her a look. "You loaded for big game?"

"You never know what you'll run into."

The deli on Central was a few blocks from the Fourth Avenue Jail. It was standard fast food design—red metal tables with attached black bench seats. The off-white ceramic floor tile and stained grout showed signs of heavy foot traffic. The soda station looked like a war zone; cups, straws, lids strewn over the counter, and puddles of various liquids on the floor screamed for a mop and bucket. All of it bore testimony to a frantic surge earlier during lunchtime. Even the counter staff looked haggard. But the place was quiet now, with only a few stragglers at the odd table here and there. It smelled like salami and fresh-baked bread.

Diego sat at a table with a dubious-looking fellow who was busy working on a steak sandwich, chips, and a huge soda. A second sandwich sat on a plate at the ready, still wrapped.

Diego stood. "Eddie. Jordan. This is Al Shetland."

Shetland acknowledged them with a loud grunt, but his attention to the sandwich didn't flag for a second.

Jordan couldn't take her eyes off him. He looked like the type of man who'd just as soon knock you down as ask you to step aside—the no nonsense, strictly business, let's get it over type, overly familiar with crime and violence. His build was average with the exception of his chest and arms, which were muscled and overly developed; it was where he gave the impression of brutality. His face was unremarkable, with the exception of his dark eyes. They looked like shark's eyes, flat and beady, with hardly any discernible white.

Diego sat back down with Al on his left. Eddie and Jordan took the chairs across from them. Jordan had to breathe through her mouth and fight the urge to bolt. Shetland smelled like a goat.

They all just sat there watching Shetland make the most of his meal, going so far as to lick the wrappers.

After he wiped his mouth and picked off the pieces of napkin stuck to his bristle, he folded his hands on the table and smiled. The effort was pleasant enough, but his mouth was the only part of his face participating in the smile. The full effect was pretty creepy.

"Al, Eddie and Jordan have questions for you about a heist."

"How may I assist you?" He spoke with a lilt, in unusual patterns, like an actor in a play. "My acquaintance Diego here, a truly fine gentleman, posted my bail and got my derriere out of lockup. He desires I talk to you? I talk to you." Al reached around Diego's shoulders and gave him a little hug.

Diego visibly tried not to jerk away.

Eddie dove right in. "I'm going to ask you a few questions about your brother, Owen."

Shetland nodded sadly. "My brother was a misguided soul, Mr. Marino."

Jordan said, "We're sorry for your loss, Al."

Al shrugged in an exaggerated way so his shoulders rose to his earlobes. "My brother was involved with many not-so-pleasant people. I'm surprised he lived as long as he did."

Al's beady eyes slid Jordan's way as she asked, "Do you know anyone in Owen's organization—anyone working for him who might be out for revenge?"

"No. Nobody in his right mind would aspire to revenge my brother. The world's a better place without him in it."

Jordan looked at Eddie and shook her head. Dead end. A total waste of time. It was obvious Al wasn't out to avenge his brother and didn't think anyone else would bother. Time to look under another rock for the killer.

Shetland looked at each of their faces in turn. "Well then, folks, I need to excuse myself now. I ate a lot, you know. A fellow doesn't eat much for a day or two then has a beautiful meal like this, he needs to excuse himself."

Jordan stood, but Eddie stayed where he was. He didn't even seem to mind sitting near the oh-so-fragrant Mr. Al Shetland.

"One more thing, Mr. Shetland," Eddie began.

"Just Al."

"Al, where were you on Wednesday night?"

Al's dark gaze softened. "I was in lock-up, Mr. Marino, and I can't begin to tell you how appreciative I am your illustrious firm sprang for my bail. If there's anything I can do for you—"

"If I need anything, Al, you'll be the first one I call." Eddie turned his hand palm up to display a folded hundred-dollar bill. "I thought you might need a little spare change."

Al seemed to like the idea of spare change, offering up another of those bizarre mechanical smiles. "Hey, man." He took the bill from Eddie and snapped it. "Like I always say, change is good for all."

Chapter 12

~

IT WAS LATE AFTERNOON on Tuesday by the time they reached the agency digs in North Scottsdale.

Tank met them in the front room. "I got something."

They went to the back room where monitors, computers, and other hi-tech gadgets allowed them to eavesdrop on the general public. Eddie's toned-down version of the NSA.

While Jordan and Eddie circled to stand behind him, Tank brought up a video of a late-model Camry stopped in the roundabout in front of the Arizona Heritage Museum. An older Accord came up behind it, never slowed or braked, and smashed into the rear of the Camry. The Camry was shoved forward and sideways. The Accord's hood looked like a broken accordion.

Both drivers got out of their cars. The guy in the Camry wore a heavy leather jacket and a motorcycle helmet he removed and tossed in the front seat. The Accord driver also got out of the car, dusting himself off.

"Powder," Tank said. "Airbag."

The two drivers stood in the middle of the road a few minutes until the Honda guy returned to his car and drove slowly away, steam rising from under the hood. The other guy also went back to his car and drove away. It didn't appear as if a single word passed between them.

"Staged," Tank said.

"Ya think?" Eddie mused.

"One more thing here." Tank adjusted the angle to show a shot of the museum entrance.

Jordan's hand rose to her mouth. "Oh, God," she said. "Muggs."

He stood behind the glass door panels, watching the street scene. After a minute, he turned away.

It was like seeing a ghost. The impact was intense. No one spoke for several minutes until Tank said, "Got something else for you guys."

He took a minute, opened a second video file, and froze a shot of a man at a table on a café patio. He sat head and shoulders taller than everyone else there. A laptop was open in front of him.

He zoomed in for a close-up. "This is from two days before the robbery. Footage from the wine bar across the street from Arizona Heritage Museum."

Eddie spoke softly. "I might know that guy. Unfreeze it."

The man in question stood. "Wow," Jordan said. "Tall dude."

Eddie nodded. "Six foot seven. Palmer Jacoby, top system man in the state, maybe the country, maybe even the world. Dollars to doughnuts he disabled security at the museum."

"So that's Palmer Jacoby." Tank's voice held a certain amount of admiration. He turned to Jordan. "Jacoby's the polar opposite of Eddie. Eddie sets up the systems. Jacoby tears 'em down." Tank zoomed in on Jacoby's face.

Jordan bent for a closer look. Jacoby wore an old-fashioned plaid driving cap pulled down a bit onto his brow. His face was pleasant and ordinary. Only his height was unusual. "Hard for a guy like that to keep a low profile," Jordan remarked. "Wouldn't mistake him in a lineup."

"If you got the chance," Eddie said. "Jacoby's out of London, but he's worked in the States twenty-five, thirty years. As far as I know, he's never been caught. The man's a legend."

EVERY OTHER TUESDAY AFTERNOON, the Canasta Cuties held court at Rachel and Sarah Abromowitz's house in the game room, which was crowded with card tables, dart boards, a foosball table, and no less than two of just about every electronic game box on the market in front of an eight foot flat screen. The Abromowitz girls did love to party.

After Jordan was introduced to the fourteen members of the canasta club, she declined sangria and finger sandwiches and asked to meet with the two sisters privately.

They led her into the elaborate sitting room at the front of the house where they all sank into the most comfortable sofas Jordan had ever experienced.

"So wonderful to hear from you, my dear," Rachel began, "what do you have for us? Have you recovered the coins?"

"Not yet," Jordan said, "but I wanted to bring you up to date. We have a source in Tucson that might lead us to the—"

Sarah interrupted. "The perp?"

Jordan suppressed a smile. "Yes, Miss Abromowitz. Perp. I see you know your criminology terms."

Rachel applauded. "Bravo, Sarah, bravo."

Sarah blushed and said, "*Castle* and *Blue Bloods*."

"We also are in the process of identifying one of the criminals—a man who's known to be a security systems expert. We believe he can lead us to the killer and the location of the coins."

The two beamed at her. "Excellent, dearest Jordan," Rachel said. "Your mother must be ever so proud of your work."

"Yes," Jordan said, "she must be."

Chapter 13

~

IT WAS LATE WEDNESDAY morning. Muggs had been gone just shy of a week.

Mary Welsh called the Camelback corridor in central Phoenix one of the few decent neighborhoods. Jordan called it the ritzy part of town, literally. The Ritz Carlton was located at 24th Street and Camelback Road. Right behind it stood the condo complex where Palmer Jacoby lived—twelve stories of stone slabs, stained concrete, steel and glass.

Eddie parked in the underground garage by the movie theater and they walked over to the high-rise. In keeping with the neighborhood, the building housed a luxurious lobby with a plush seating area near the elevators. A sturdy young man in a white shirt and black trousers stood watch behind the desk.

"Gina didn't have the unit number." Eddie reached for his wallet. "Let's see if a little grease at the front desk won't get us what we want."

Jordan sized up the good-looking young man—early twenties, probably a college student, short, well-trimmed hair, clean-cut, baby face. She smiled, tugged her shirt down so her cleavage was better exposed, sucked in her stomach and stayed

Eddie with her hand. "I got this one, moneybags."

She called it her persuasive seduction mode, but considered retagging it her Sofia Vercelli act. It involved languid swaying of her arms, shoulders pulled back, breasts thrust out, lips on full pout, and hips pumping like pistons. It was, for all intents and purposes, a cartoon—more Jessica Rabbit than Jordan Welsh—but it always seemed to work.

"Hi, there," she said, daring to add, "handsome."

The young man looked up from what appeared to be a delivery log. His eyes started on her face then dropped to her exposed cleavage.

Perfect. Eat your heart out, Marino.

"How," he cleared his throat, "may I help you?"

"Can y'all do me a favor, sugar?" It was a soprano version of Tank's Louisiana drawl. "A tall, cool drink of water by the name of Palmer Jacoby lives here, right?"

The young man's jaw hung open. She had him. She leaned her arms on the counter. This was way too much fun to be considered work. "Could y'all tell me what floor he lives on? I'd like to surprise him."

The young man smiled, displaying teeth his parents probably paid thousands to have straightened to perfection. "I won't tell you."

She pulled away. No way. She had this guy panting. *He won't tell me? What's up with that?*

His eyes moved beyond her and settled admiringly on Eddie. "But I'll tell him anything he wants to know. Anything at all."

Jordan turned as Eddie grinned, straightened his shoulders and joined her at the reception desk. "Don't worry, babe. I got this one."

THE RED TAG SALE at Saks Fifth Avenue drew shoppers from far and wide, including a six-foot-seven British thief named Palmer Jacoby, according to Eddie's newfound BFF, the receptionist at Jacoby's condo building.

They found Jacoby in front of a mirror at the hat counter modeling a charcoal gray fedora with a blue-striped band and small pheasant feather. Dapper. By his pose it was obvious he was aware of the fine figure he cut in his gray cord sport coat and black silky trousers. The shirt under the cord jacket was bright blue. A gray plaid driving cap lay on the counter. It was the hat Jordan remembered from the video. Three big, black and white Saks shopping bags sat on the floor at his feet.

He paid for the hat, left the store, and crossed the grassy courtyard. An escalator carried him to the second story and the Henry the Eighth Pub and Eatery. Jordan had been there at least three times before—twice for lunch when shopping at the mall with her sister Kate and their mother, and once when she met a potential client for late afternoon drinks. The place didn't look much like a pub but was still loaded with British atmosphere. The dining area was well-furnished with round hardwood tables and captain's chairs. The British-racing-green walls were decorated with hunting prints of foxes and hounds, elegant steeds, and men in red jackets. The richly polished bar and backbar could have been lifted straight from an uptown London pub. The smell of hops and bar food assaulted Jordan, and her stomach rumbled as she remembered the excellent shepherd's pie served there.

Eddie and Jordan waited outside a few minutes then went in and walked straight up to Palmer's table. Palmer looked up. A shadow crossed his face before he smiled graciously. "Eddie Marino, as I live and breathe."

"Big day at the mall, Palmer?"

A shrug. "Every man has his vice." His gaze shifted to Jordan. "Aren't you going to introduce me to yours?" His accent was upper-crust London.

What a smoothie. Judging from the gray at his temples, he was around fifty. His face was nice, not handsome, but nice. His smile seemed to switch off and on easily, bringing dimples with it. The driving cap was gone, probably in one of the shopping bags. She could see now he had a high forehead made more prominent by the receding hairline. According to Eddie and Tank, Palmer Jacoby was a notorious thief, but Jordan liked him in spite of it.

Eddie pulled out a chair and held it. Jordan sat. Eddie took the chair beside her.

Palmer looked from one to the other. "Please," he said sarcastically, "why don't you join me?"

A waiter delivered a tall schooner of dark ale. Palmer raised it to them then drank. Foam lined his upper lip. "Ah, yes, Guinness stout. Breakfast of champions." He sighed. "I wager this isn't purely a social visit, eh, Eddie?"

A stout man in a navy blue blazer approached the table. "Jordan Welsh. It's good to see you again. It's been a while."

"Hello, Charles. Nice to see you as well. This is my partner, Eddie Marino, and …?" She looked at Palmer.

He stood and thrust out his hand. "Palmer Jacoby. A pleasure to meet you, Charles."

More niceties exchanged. Then Charles said, "I'll leave you to enjoy your lunch. If you need anything, Jordan, let me know."

She nodded. "Thanks, Charles."

"My best to your folks."

"Of course."

As Charles walked away, Palmer turned to her. "I'm impressed, Miss Welsh. I eat at this establishment several times a week, and the manager's never come over and said how glad he was to see me here. Of course, I'm not statuesque and beautiful, but still—"

Eddie interrupted. "Everyone knows Jordan."

Jordan shrugged it off. "It's a small town when you get right down to it."

"Absolutely. Only the fifth largest city in America." Another pleasant smile from one of the world's foremost thieves.

"Palmer, we're here to ask you a few questions about a place hit in downtown Scottsdale a week ago today. The Arizona Heritage Museum," Eddie said.

Palmer's expression was one of inquisitive interest. "You'll have to elaborate, my friend. You know I don't follow the news. Depressing for the most part."

Eddie nodded grimly. "Yeah. I remember that about you. Yesterday is past. Tomorrow is coming. Today is what matters. Right, Palmer?"

Another hit on the Guinness. Another smile.

Jordan felt left out of the loop. Why the heck were they talking in circles? She sat back and let Eddie take the lead.

"Palmer, there are certain things people in our line of work don't discuss openly, or at least in specific terms."

Jacoby nodded.

Eddie went on. "I know this might be one of them."

Our line of work? Eddie was in the same line of work as she. Wasn't he?

"Very well, you two. Let me just say, if I had knowledge of such a caper, I wouldn't be in a position to discuss it."

Eddie nodded.

"I'm a retired crime reconstruction agent living out my waning years in the warm Arizona sun."

"Mm-hmm, and I'm heir to the British crown," Eddie said.

Palmer smiled yet again. "I always knew there was something special about you, Eddie, aside from those remarkable, complicated security systems you build."

"Why thank you, Palmer. Let me just return the compliment and say I've always admired how quickly you can take them apart."

Jordan had no patience for the mutual admiration club, especially since Palmer Jacoby was someone from Eddie's dark past. "We have a special interest here, Mr. Jacoby. We were on the job that night. It was our duty to protect the items stolen from the museum, and it was our friend and employee who was murdered."

Palmer couldn't hide his reaction this time. The color drained from his face. His brows drew together. "Someone was killed?"

Eddie said slowly, "Sometimes it pays to watch the news. It was Muggs Baxter."

Palmer sucked in his breath. He blinked. Tears glistened in his eyes. Jordan looked away. It was obvious Palmer Jacoby had no previous knowledge of Muggs's murder. Nobody was that good an actor.

Chapter 14

~

IT WAS ABOUT FOUR o'clock by the time they left Jacoby, and rush hour was in full swing. The junction where State Route 51 ended and traffic merged onto 101 west was a parking lot.

Eddie and Jordan rolled forward a few feet at a time.

"I know you don't approve of the way I handled things with Palmer," Eddie said. "There's a protocol, a kind of honor among thieves. We don't press. If Palmer gave up anything about what went down on one of his jobs, he'd never work in this state, let alone this town, again. He's too old to plan this stuff on his own anymore and his reputation has to be rock solid or he won't be hired."

She stared at him. "*We* don't press?"

He glanced at her as they finally moved onto the 101 and into the HOV lane. "Did you want to get anything out of him or not? Unless I spoke to him just right, he'd have clammed up on us."

"Oh, I see." She slanted a hard look in his direction. "And because you pussyfooted around with him, he gave us *so* much. As far as I could see, the visit was a waste of time." She shuddered. "You have no idea how much it scares me when

I see you consorting with these people. You fit back in so seamlessly."

"Fit in? What are you talking about? I don't fit in with them. Not anymore."

"It doesn't always seem that way."

"It's not all bad, you know," he said. "There are advantages to having a partner who knows what buttons to push, what doors to open to help the company, our company, when the timing is right."

Jordan could only agree with him. "I just wish you weren't so comfortable pushing those buttons."

The owner of Westside Trampoline Center had called the office and asked them to come around and tweak the surveillance system. Apparently a kid had bounced off cockeyed, the camera had missed it, and now the parents were suing for negligence. To accommodate them, their client closed early. Eddie used the key provided to the firm to open the door then enter the alarm code.

Even though they were trying to focus all their resources on the Arizona Heritage Museum burglary and Muggs's murder, their client insisted this was somewhat of an emergency. Whether it was or not, they felt obligated to tend to it.

The place was located in a strip mall in a space previously occupied by a grocery. A service desk, a snack bar, and a small locker room took up the front area.

The actual entrance leading to the trampolines was an open archway.

Eddie stopped before entering and toed the heel of his boots. "Shoes off, Miss Jordan."

She gave him a look.

"I mean it. Those pads cost a fortune. We don't want to pay for the punctures those shoes would make."

She slipped off her shoes, Joan and David teal suede kitten heels. "There's no one else here, right?"

"What? You worried someone's going to walk off with your shoes?" Eddie held up a hand as if making a vow. "If they disappear, I promise to buy you a new pair."

The main room was like a video game board, with a grid made up of lemon yellow pads and bright blue trampoline net covering the floor and climbing the walls. Jordan felt like an avatar in *Tron*.

They crossed all the way to the back and passed through another big open archway to a service area. Eddie turned on all the monitors and video cameras. It took only a minute for everything to come online. He stood, chin in hand. "Four, seven, and twelve need just a bit of a tweak." He grabbed a ten-foot long aluminum pole with a pistol grip and spring-operated claw.

They returned to the main room, their feet sinking into the vinyl-covered foam mats.

Eddie stood beneath the camera marked four, took hold of it with the claw and shifted it ever so slightly.

Jordan craned her neck. "How's Mama Rose doing?"

"Okay, I guess." He shrugged. "How do you mean?"

"You know, about Muggs."

"I'm guessing it hurts her some." His voice was soft.

"At least she's not badgering you to quit the business and take up the cloth."

He didn't look at her. "Your mom?"

"Who else?" she said. Something had been bothering Jordan. "Why do you think Mama Rose was so adamant it's the mob?"

"Mama blames the mob for a lot of my trouble. Back when we were kids …." He repeated the angle adjustment on number seven.

"Kids? You and who else?"

"Me, Muggs, Tank, and Diego, we got in some major trouble. Wrong place, wrong time, wrong people. They hauled us in front of a judge, who was sick and tired of seeing Cleveland kids. He said, 'You choose. Serve your time in jail or in the military." Didn't seem like we had much choice. Tank and I went with the Army. Muggs and Diego joined the Marines."

"The few, the proud?" Jordan asked. She knew all this from a previous conversation with Gina, but it was good to hear it from Eddie.

"Yeah, those Marines. Anyway, Mama always believed the mob was the reason we got sent away. I can see her point. No love lost there."

Camera number twelve was shoved to the left.

"Was it? The mob, I mean. Were you guys in trouble because of the mob?"

Eddie turned away and headed back to the service room. "No. Not that time anyway, but we all did work for Anthony Vercelli. Before he moved his main operation out here."

"What is it between the two of you?"

He put the pole back in the utility closet and sat down in front of the monitors. "Who? Me and Vercelli? Is this going to be a replay of the talk we had when you found out I used to work for him?"

"When we went to his place last year about the fraud case, it was like you didn't want to hurt his feelings or something and you said you—"

"Respected him."

"I still don't understand."

"It's still complicated." He ran through all fifteen cameras, switching back and forth using the remote.

"Don't, Marino. Don't give me the runaround. Your sleight of hand routine."

"Okay." He spun the chair and faced her. "Here it is. The man helped me. He gave me work when I needed it most. Without him, me, my sister and my sweet mama would have been out on the street." He stood. "We're done working here."

She followed him back into the main room. "He took advantage of a naïve kid," she said.

"Not so naïve if I'm honest, but you can believe what you

want. Because of our history, I still have a certain allegiance to him."

She stopped in the middle of the room.

He stopped a few feet in front, his back to her. His shoulders slumped. Eddie had never liked talking about his time with the mob. He turned, came back to her and waited, arms folded more in submission than anger or resistance. "Go for it, Jordan. Get it out of your system."

She dove in. "When you were moving among Vercelli's people on the Foundation case, I didn't worry about it. You were out of there, gone. Done with them. Whatever drove you away, kept you away. But today you talked to Jacoby like you were birds of a feather. And here comes this Sofia person sniffing around you, and I don't know anything about her, and …." Her voice broke.

He put his arm around her waist and drew her to him. "Okay, partner, here it is. I talked to Jacoby like that because otherwise there wouldn't have been any dialogue with him. I'm not going back to that life. Not now, not ever. And Sofia? You got nothing to worry about there."

"I don't?" She hated how small and insecure her voice sounded.

"When Sofia learned I was leaving her father's organization, she told me she was pregnant. She told me it was mine. I was in love with her, or thought I was, and I believed what she said. I went to Anthony and asked for his permission to marry her. The old man looked me straight in the eye and said it would be his honor to have me for a son. But she lied. There was no baby. She had already told another man before me the same thing to keep him." It seemed to drain him.

She was afraid to hear the answer, but she had to ask. *Please let him lie if he has to.* "Do you still love her?"

"I'm not sure I ever did. Anyway, are you crazy? How could I love her after I've been with you? You're the hot ticket, Jordan."

"Good answer, Marino." She believed him, maybe just

because she wanted to. "Just one more thing before we leave."

"What?"

"Let's take those trampolines for a spin."

She took a running start and leapt onto the nearest one, ricocheted off and bounced back up.

He followed suit. They fell down together, rolling and groping like teenagers in the backseat of a car at the local make-out spot, but stopped before things got out of hand.

Back at the front entrance, Jordan slipped her shoes on and turned to Eddie. "You did turn off those surveillance cameras, right?"

Chapter 15

❧

THURSDAY MORNING, ALL OF Shea Investigations along with Mama Rose and her beau Marky Mark gathered at the Shea offices to caravan to Flagstaff and the Coconino National Forest.

Beneath the splendor of the San Francisco Peaks and standing among the Ponderosa Pines, Eddie, Jordan, Tank, Diego, Gina, Mama Rose, and Marky Mark listened to the mournful wail of a lone bagpiper playing "Amazing Grace" and said one final goodbye to a good friend.

Rose was inconsolable, sobbing out loud as she pulled one fancy lace hanky after another from her handbag.

Tank and Diego turned away, overcome with strong emotion, but Eddie put one arm around Jordan, the other around his mother and wept openly.

Jordan's heart ached for them all, especially for Eddie, but she tried to stay strong. She, too, loved Muggs like a brother, even if the softest spot in her heart was for Tank. His sweet Southern ways had always charmed her, and his vigilance had kept her safe in the past.

After casting Muggs's ashes in the crisp mountain breeze,

they retired one and all, including the Scottish piper, to the warm comfort of the Shade Tree Lounge at the San Francisco Peaks Hotel. The lodge atmosphere was enhanced by the cheerful blaze in the stone fireplace and heavy wood beams crossing the vaulted ceiling.

Pizza, wings, and nachos were the staples of Muggs's diet and the chosen fare for the evening activities, plus as many bottles of Johnny Walker Black as the eight of them could consume. While the servers pretended to look the other way, even Gina was allowed to indulge due to the occasion.

By eight thirty, every one of them had slurred his or her most outrageous story about the man who had been Marvin "Muggs" Baxter. Eddie described the time four screaming teenage girls chased him into the men's room at a downtown hotel, yelling "Thor!"—convinced he was Chris Hemsworth, the actor. Muggs barricaded himself in one of the stalls and called 911.

Tank told them about the time he and Muggs returned to their parked car in the PD parking lot to discover no fewer than a dozen sticky notes with phone numbers and call me messages attached to the windshield. Most of the names were female, but a few were definitely male.

Just before heading for their rooms, Eddie stood one final time. They all filled their glasses as he prepared to eulogize his friend.

"Muggs was the kind of guy who always had your back. You never worried because you just knew he'd be there. He was good at what he did. Of everyone I know, he always had the cleanest gun chamber, and most well-conditioned hair."

Tank moaned, "I always loved his hair," and sobbed.

Eddie and Diego nodded their agreement.

"Focus, Eddie," Jordan said softly.

"Muggs was a great dresser." Diego's contribution.

But Eddie disagreed. "Give me a break. Those shirts? Guy looked like he belonged in Margaritaville. Women dug him, though."

Not a single other word was added, nor were more needed.

On cue, the bagpiper broke out into Muggs's favorite song, the Four Seasons' "Oh, What a Night," which sounded a bit odd on bagpipes, but no one cared.

THEY RETURNED TO SCOTTSDALE the next morning.

Eddie dropped Jordan at her place then went home to shower. He arrived at the office at noon, wearing sunglasses and a Cleveland Indians baseball cap. When he took off the glasses, his bloodshot eyes told the tale of overindulgence the night before.

Jordan had beaten him to the office by a good hour.

He headed straight to Gina's desk.

"You know that special project I had you working on? How's it coming?"

"Great timing, Uncle Eddie. I just printed it out for you." Gina reached behind her and removed three sheets from the printer tray.

Eddie snatched the sheets from her hand and dragged himself into his office.

Jordan turned to her office manager. The question in her mind didn't make it to her lips before Gina replied, "It's a background check on Mark Garrity." Gina rolled her eyes at Jordan.

Oh, swell, how the heck would they break it to Rose if the guy turned out to be a creep? "How'd it come out?"

Gina shrugged. "The dude looks okay to me ... on paper anyway."

Jordan moseyed into Eddie's office. "So, how bad is it?"

Eddie sat in one of the armchairs in front of his desk.

He stuck out a foot, hooked the lower rung of the other chair and pulled it up beside him. She sat in it, and he leaned over to share the pages.

"You know," she said, scanning the data, "if you hadn't done this, I might have."

"Damn right, but I can't tell you how relieved I am there's nothing terrible here. I didn't know how I was going to break it to Mama if we came up with anything."

Jordan agreed with a nod, her eyes skimming the printed sheets.

Gina did a good job. Everything seemed to be listed there, things Jordan wanted to know about Mark, and a few things she didn't want to know about him.

Eddie said, "Guy was born in Queens. He's sixty-two."

"Oooh," Jordan said. "Mama Rose is a cradle robber."

"You call a five-year difference robbing the cradle?" Eddie massaged his temples. "Thing is, guy's been married before—three times before. Divorced twice, widowed once, cancer. At least he didn't off her. That's a plus."

A plus? Only Eddie would put it that way.

"You know," Eddie began, "I was halfway hoping the movie thing was a con. But it's legit. He produced a half dozen low budget films in Spain. None of them were what you'd call blockbusters, but they didn't lose a lot either."

"So he's not after Mama Rose's royalties?"

Eddie sighed. "As much as I hate to admit it, I don't think so. The guy looks clean."

Jordan smiled and laid a sympathetic hand on Eddie's arm. "So you think the old boy's in love?"

Eddie looked at her.

She shrugged. "Well, why not? Mama Rose is quite a dish. But I do have one question."

"What?"

She pointed at a notation at the bottom of the report. It was in red bold print and surrounded by asterisks.

"Oh." Eddie sounded embarrassed. "Looks like Gina took me literally."

Jordan cocked her head. "What does it mean? Little blue pill prescription in nightstand at hotel? Ralph Lauren silk boxers?"

He shrugged. "I told her I wanted to know everything about the guy, even …."

She sighed. "Why am I not surprised?"

Chapter 16

~

FRIDAY MORNING AND NOT a clue in sight. Eddie's phone rang—generic.

Lucky Louie's voice came over the line, so high-pitched that Eddie didn't even recognize it.

"*Señor* Marino, it's Luis Martinez. You know ... Lucky?"

"Oh." Eddie's heart rate picked up. "You have something for me?"

"Look, holmes, something you should know." Luis spoke so quickly Eddie could barely understand him. Something sure had him riled. "There's people got a stake in this deal you don't want to be messing with. Bad people."

Eddie wished he were there to shake Luis and make him get to the point. "What people?"

"I don't want to say—

"Oh, come on. Louie. I don't have time for this."

Louie grew quiet. Eddie could hear him breathing heavily over the phone all the way from South Tucson. "It's the cartels." Eddie caught his breath. "I found out the cartels are tied up in this deal with the stolen coins."

Eddie stood and kicked back his chair. "Tell me what you know."

"Look. I can't talk about it now. Not on the phone. But I'm afraid. I'm really afraid, man. I'm gonna have to pull in that favor we talked about. You gotta promise me if I help you, you'll make sure your friends got my back, man."

JORDAN WAS ON THE phone with Steve Keegan. Keegan had a private firm, Keegan and Associates Fire Consultants.

"Hi, missy," he said. "I heard about your man, Muggs Baxter. Only met him a time or two, but he seemed like a regular guy. Condolences."

"Thanks, Steve," she said. "We miss him. I called to see if you have anything new on the nightclub case."

"The forensics team is still working on the evidence gathered from the scene. Looks like the accelerant was gasoline. I may be old and forgetful, but even a kid could figure that out in a minute and a half."

"We already know this Overton character, the club owner, was knee deep in some Ponzi scheme," she said. "Losses in the millions. Torching his own club was his way of raising cash. Right? So we're getting close to bagging the firebug?"

Jokers Wild, a nightclub in South Phoenix, had burned to the ground six weeks earlier. Due to suspicious circumstances and the owner's shaky financial situation, an insurance company they'd worked with in the past hired Shea Investigations to look into the matter. Jordan had called Steve, who was the go-to arson guy statewide. His reputation spanned thirty years, which put him in his late fifties or early sixties. He was the best in the business. Nothing ever seemed to get by him.

"We are, indeed, closing in," he said. "I should have a more complete report on the scene in a week or ten days. I'll keep you posted."

"Thanks."

At least she had some good news on one of their cases. Too

bad the other one—the one that mattered—seemed to be stalled. Even the Abromowitz sisters were getting antsy for some good news. They'd left three voicemails over the past couple of days inquiring as to their progress. It was now ten days since the museum robbery, and Jordan didn't really have anything to tell them. She had lucked out. When she returned the call, they didn't pick up, allowing her to simply leave a message. "Things are coming along. We have a few really good leads."

The door to Jordan's office flew open, and Eddie blew in like a windstorm. "I just got off the phone with Diego's contact in Tucson."

"Luis Martinez?" she asked.

He was out of breath. "Lucky Louie. He has a lead that could blow this wide open. I gotta go down there."

"Right now?"

"Tomorrow."

He told her Martinez had discovered a connection between the Mexican drug cartels and the Dahlonega coins.

"What connection?" she prodded.

"He never said. He's scared to death, Jordan. That's why I have to go."

The drug cartels. She swallowed hard. This was beyond serious. She was scared, but Eddie seemed energized by it all.

He went on. "And it has to be tomorrow because Louie told the guy with the coins he had a couple of people who'd take 'em all—the whole kit and caboodle. You know, just to get our guy back in the store. It's going down tomorrow, Saturday, at one. I'm going to get there a little early to set up surveillance."

"What time are we leaving?"

"Not 'we.' Me. I'll go first. You can drive with Tank and Diego later."

She bristled. Would she ever break him of the habit of trying to keep her stuck up on a pedestal, out of harm's way? "It's my reputation on the line here, too. Did you think I didn't have a vested interest in recovering the coins? And besides, I may not have known Muggs as long as you did, but I loved him. Don't shut me out."

"Who said anything about shutting you out? If you come down later, by the time you get there it'll just be a matter of getting into position and waiting for the bust to go down."

"You sure?"

"I'm always sure, baby cakes."

She got up, went around behind him and circled him with her arms. He smelled clean and woodsy. Aramis, just the hint of it.

"What time are you picking me up tonight?"

"What time's the engagement party again?" His voice was husky.

"Seven."

"I'll be there at five. That'll give us a little time to … talk. Or something." He kissed her, hard.

His blood was up over this Martinez thing, and when Eddie's blood was up, she could count on an energetic evening.

She breathed against his mouth. "I just love it when we talk … or something."

MARY AND BEN WELSH lived in Troon, in North Scottsdale. The area was famous for sports icons, renowned authors, movie personalities, and rock stars. Nestled among boulders and the grassy golf course, the houses were all custom-built and some of the richest real estate in Arizona.

The Welsh home was four thousand square feet of opulence and excess. Mary had it furnished and decorated in a similar way to their place in Lake Forest, with antiques and imports mixed with rich tones—French renaissance with a Southwestern twist.

Over the top, according to Jordan and her sister Kate, but when you walked in, there was no doubt Mary Welsh lived there. Her fingerprints were everywhere, from the Louis XIV sink pedestal to the brass-studded leather Mexican bar stools at the kitchen counter. God forbid anyone pointed out the incongruities to her.

Jordan and Eddie showed up at seven fifteen. The engagement party was already in full swing. They were just a tad late due to their intense and satisfying *conversation* and the subsequent need to shower afterward.

The valley's glitterati were there in full force—about a hundred, all told. Jordan had to hand it to her mother. Only Mary Welsh, reigning queen of Chicago society and heiress apparent in the Valley of the Sun, could assemble such a star-studded event in a week's time.

Food and wine from the family's restaurant, arranged by Jordan's brother Alec, would be served at eight in a big party tent set up in the back patio area. Two bartenders also borrowed from her parents' restaurant mixed, served, and entertained the guests while servers circulated with trays of hors d'oeuvres.

From the back of the house, Mary shuffled to meet them, hampered by flopping three-inch mule sandals that clicked against the tile with each step. There was a bloom on her cheeks and a sloshing champagne flute in each hand.

Rose followed along behind her, a vision in a cream-colored, silk pantsuit with a silk cami the color of storm clouds. Silvery pumps studded with sparkling stones peeked from under the hem of her pants. Four strands of pearls circled her neck. Her salt and pepper hair was immaculately styled. Gone was the frizzy disarray she usually sported. Her makeup was understated.

Jordan took her hand. "Rose, you're stunning."

Mary, who was normally the definition of polite society, giggled. "Can you believe it, Jordan? Rose is wearing a Gucci suit!"

Jordan waited for Eddie to compliment both women, but instead he stood, hands in his pockets, studying the tops of his shoes.

She nudged him. "Eddie?"

He looked up. "Huh?"

"Doesn't your mom look pretty tonight?"

He seemed to wake up. "Oh, yeah. Gorgeous. You, too, Mary. Both of you ladies. Just gorgeous."

She leaned over and whispered in his ear, "You okay?"

He nodded, still smiling at his mother and Mary. "Yeah, just thinking about tomorrow."

Jordan couldn't say she blamed him. The trip down to Tucson would be interesting, to say the least.

Jordan put her arm around Rose's shoulders. "Come on, Mama Rose. I'll buy you a drink."

Alec, his wife, Caroline, and their twin daughters scoped out the appetizer table in the great room. Both girls, bound for kindergarten in the fall, were dressed in frilly pink princess dresses. They looked like miniatures of their mother, an attractive French woman with big brown eyes and lush dark hair.

Caroline and the girls hovered by the serving table where the twins had launched an attack against a cheese platter.

Alec put his arm around Jordan and bussed her cheek. "Hey, baby sister. How's the PI biz treating you?"

From behind them came, "*Au contraire*, Alec, not the question of the night."

They turned to see the middle Welsh offspring—Jordan's sister, Kate—with Dave Clark, the lovable bank manager she'd been seriously dating for several months. Dave headed for the serving table where he assisted the twins in the assault on the Brie.

With pale blue eyes and golden brown hair like Alec's, Kate was all Welsh. Jordan and her mother sported the copper hair and hazel eyes of the Irish O'Connells.

"Then what is the important question of the night?" Alec asked.

Kate laughed. "Has Mother had her first meltdown yet?"

"Not yet," Jordan said, "but then she's yet to have one like the time back at …"

They raised their voices an octave to spout, "… *Sacré Coeur* School for Young Ladies."

Kate huffed. "You nearly got me expelled."

"Me?" Jordan feigned outrage. "It was all your idea."

They both knew it wasn't. Saint Katherine, as Jordan often called her older sister, not only wouldn't think up the mischief they got into, she couldn't. It wasn't in her genes.

When Jordan was in her sophomore year, Abraham Lipchitz, from the Hasidic Yeshiva Academy for Exceptional Boys down the street from *Sacré Coeur*, gave her two joints of a strain he called Purple Haze. Not only had she not smoked them, she'd left them in her gym locker. It was Friday night and Jordan was paranoid the joints would be found. Silver-tongued devil that she was, Jordan convinced Kate to help her break into the school to retrieve them.

Kate was terrified, but she loaded her little sister into her 1998 red Mustang convertible and drove down to the high school. They circled the building until they spotted an open window, crawled in and made their way to the gym. Kate cursed a blue streak the entire time, words Jordan had never heard before or since.

The girls' locker room was suspiciously steamy when the two young women snuck in at eight thirty p.m. Who the hell would be taking a shower in the girls' gym at the high school? Well, come to find out, it was Mr. Pachnowski, the biology teacher, and Miss Mackenzie, the women's tennis coach, getting it on in the shower.

They didn't want to look, but couldn't look away. Katie slipped on the wet concrete and went down. Coach Mackenzie shrieked and came charging out. Professor Pachnowski cowered in the corner, clutching the shower curtain to his privates—too little, too late, literally.

The end result was that Miss Mackenzie found the joints and

kicked Jordan off the tennis team. But when she tried to get Jordan and Kate expelled, Kate couldn't stand it and narced out the two teachers. Both were eventually let go. Katie got off with a stern reprimand. Jordan sat out eight weeks of her sophomore year, which she wouldn't have considered punishment except it meant spending eight weeks of quarantine at home with Mary. Her mother was humiliated beyond words and spent nearly the entire eight weeks, screeching at Jordan about how she was turning into a juvenile delinquent and might have to join the … wait for it … Merchant Marine. It took Mary nearly all of Jordan's remaining two and half years at *Sacré Coeur* to get over it.

"Yep." Katie rolled her eyes. "Nearly went thermonuclear all right. She spent the next two months lying on the chaise in her bedroom with a cold cloth across her brow."

As if Jordan could ever forget. "Yeah, ordering me to fetch her stuff twenty-four hours a day."

And right on cue, the target of their query stopped a young man in a crisp white shirt and black trousers who was circulating a tray of canapés, to straighten his bow tie.

The three Welsh siblings stood shoulder to shoulder and sighed as Mary turned her sharp eyes in their direction. *Uh-oh. Storm front imminent.*

"Oh, swell," Alec said. "Here she comes. Is my hair sticking up or anything?"

EDDIE FOUND HIMSELF OUTSIDE on the back patio with a Dewar's on the rocks in one hand, a cigar in the other, and Marky Mark at his elbow.

He was having trouble tracking what Mark was saying. His mind was on the events that would be unfolding in the morning. Deep down he had a strong feeling this could be the turning point in the case.

"Thanks for stepping out with me." Mark sounded unsure of himself.

"No problem. What can I do for you?"

"Look, Eddie," he began slowly. "I know you aren't too crazy about the idea of me marrying your mom—"

Eddie opened his mouth to say something, but Mark held up his hand.

"No. It's okay, man, I understand. She's doing okay financially, lot of publicity. I can see where you'd figure I'm just a scumbag out to swindle her money."

"I …." Eddie searched for a way to make a denial that wasn't an outright lie.

"Something I want to show you." Mark pulled a folded document from his jacket pocket.

Eddie set his drink on the table, his cigar in the ashtray and moved over under a pillar light where he could see.

It only took a minute for him to figure out what he was looking at. "This is a—"

"Yep," Mark said. "A prenup. It basically says what's hers is hers and what's mine is hers."

Eddie stared at Mark as the man went on, "I love your mother. She's a class act. Worm like me, I don't deserve her. I've been married before. I'm not ashamed to say it because the man I was then isn't the man I am today. I may be a slow learner, but I did learn. Rose is it for me. I want to spend the rest of my life with her. All I have, I'm sharing with her. And I won't be asking for anything from her in return except the pleasure of her company."

Eddie just stood there, caught off guard by the sincerity in Mark's voice. There wasn't anything left for him to say. He stuck out his hand and Mark took it. They shook.

The only reply that came to mind was, "Welcome to the family."

Mark sighed, big and long. It was obvious he'd been expecting a different result. "I gotta say that went down easier than I expected. I figured I'd be lucky to get off without a bullet in my chest."

Eddie stared at him and swallowed hard. What had Mama been saying to him? He was a little ashamed that whatever she'd said, it was probably true.

He must have looked stunned because Mark was quick to say. "No, no. I was just messing with you."

"Oh." Eddie felt like an idiot.

"One more thing," Mark said.

"Yeah? What?"

"Now that we're friends and all, do you think you could stop calling me Marky Mark?"

Chapter 17

~

SATURDAY MORNING BROUGHT WIND to Phoenix and Scottsdale. The air was so full with yellow Palo Verde blossoms, they seemed to be raining down. Eddie pulled the Ford Ranger out of the garage and hit Interstate 10 heading south. It was a little over an hour and a half to the South Fourth Avenue location of Lucky Louie's Pawn Shop in South Tucson.

In Tucson it actually was raining, a cold spring downpour. The deep chuckholes in the empty parking lot were filled with dirty runoff. Eddie turned up the collar of his denim jacket and walked around to the back.

He mentally ticked off, item by item, what he had planned. First, lie in wait for Louie's contact to come. Second, make him talk. Third, if it turned out to be the scum who killed Muggs and took the coins, take him down. Fourth, get Martinez out of harm's way. All this he planned to do before Jordan arrived with Tank and Diego. She hadn't been far off the mark when she chewed his butt for trying to shut her out. He didn't want her anywhere near the cartel.

Both the security gate and rear door stood open. Rain

poured off the overhang, drenching him as he stared at the grisly scene.

He took a step inside, resisting the urge to shake off the water like a soaked dog as the drizzle coming in behind him ran in muddy rivulets to the two bodies face down on the concrete floor.

A few quick steps carried Eddie across the room. He knelt beside the first body and put two fingers to the carotid artery. No pulse. It was Louie's muscular bulldog he and Jordan ran into on their first trip down. The second body was a younger man, Latino. The enormous rock on his right hand identified him as the courier from Louie's security footage.

Both men had been shot in the back.

Luis Martinez was slumped over the table, bullet hole in the back of his head.

In the far corner of the room, the door to the old safe stood open. Eddie didn't need to have a look. He knew the metal box and its contents wouldn't be there.

A moment of regret passed over him. Maybe he should have come down yesterday. Maybe Martinez would still be alive. What a waste of life, and Eddie still didn't have what he needed.

A scrape. The unmistakable click of a gun being cocked. Before he could even react—

"Stand up straight. Hands on top of your head." The command came from behind him. He obeyed. "Turn around. Take your time, friend. Like an instant replay in slow-mo."

The cop's shirtsleeve said he was South Tucson PD. His gun aimed at Eddie's chest said he was in charge.

"It's not what it looks like, officer." *Get it on the record, Eddie.*

"Of course not." The cop smiled. "It never is."

SHE MUST HAVE THANKED Ann a dozen times for driving to Tucson with her. Not that it had been easy being in the car together. The topic of the conversation during most of the ninety-minute ride had centered on the obvious fact that their relationship was tricky, that there was a fine line between their strong friendship and their professional interaction.

But in the end, the detective's word had gone a long way toward getting Eddie out of the cell in South Tucson.

The cops took Eddie straight from the crime scene to lockup, where he'd been for the past three hours. When he walked out to meet Jordan, something about his wounded expression bothered her. She couldn't quite put her finger on it. He looked and smelled a lot better than when he was locked up last time.

He hugged her.

He turned to Ann and offered to shake. "Thanks, Detective Murphy. Your endorsement obviously goes a long way with these guys down here."

She ignored his hand. "If you'd brought us and the Tucson cops in on this, we could have set up a sting operation. We'd have the coins, we'd have the perp, and we wouldn't have three bodies. What were you thinking, Marino?"

Eddie had the grace to look at his feet. "Sorry."

Fifteen minutes later, the three sat down with Detectives Rico and Castro from the South Tucson PD and Pima County Sheriff's Office.

Rico, the city cop, was buff and good-looking, while Sheriff's Deputy Castro looked to be about ten years past retirement age and getting softer before Jordan's eyes.

"Lucky Louie was known to black market stolen goods to his contacts in Mexico. He's been on our watch list for a while now. This was bound to happen sooner or later," Rico said.

Castro shoved a file across the desk toward Ann. "These are his connections on the other side of the border. Since you told us about the stolen coins, we've notified agencies in Sonora to be on alert."

"Mexico? Good luck with that," Eddie muttered.

Rico said, "As far as we can tell, Mr. Marino was only fifteen minutes or so behind the killer. We think ballistics will show that the same gun shot all three. So, one guy. The security cameras were disabled with a magnetic pulse at ten fifteen. Only about five minutes later, reported gunfire sent us to the crime scene. Probably when it went down. But we'll know for sure when we get the ME's report."

Castro spread his hands. "That's it, people. We got nothing else. We're hoping anything you come up with, Detective Murphy, you'll play nice and share."

Ann stood. "We will. And you'll reciprocate?"

The cops nodded.

While Ann traded contact information with the officers, Jordan and Eddie walked out together and stood in the parking lot under a big mesquite tree while they waited for the release of Eddie's truck from impound. A couple of black-and-whites were parked in the lot. Most forces as small as South Tucson's couldn't afford to have any inactive vehicles.

The sun came out over the Tucson Mountains from behind the clouds and exploded in a double rainbow. It would be so much simpler if the Dahlonega coins were in the pot at its end.

He said quietly, "Whoever this guy is, he's dangerous. That's the second time he's blindsided me."

He cut his eyes at her, and she knew he was worried. It was what she'd seen on his face when they set him loose earlier. She was worried, too.

"I can't seem to get out in front of him," he said. "Smart. I gotta tell you it scares me some. He seems to know exactly what I'm going to do and when I'm going to do it. I don't like what that could mean."

Chapter 18

FLORENCE PRISON HAD TO be the most depressing place on the face of the planet, and after his experiences with jail cells the last couple of weeks, Eddie was freakin' delighted to be on the walk-away side of the table.

He and Diego sat waiting in the empty visitation room at a simple table-and-chairs setup that made Eddie want to order a burger. One Simon Cooper, who according to Diego's contact was the go-to guy for tattoos in the Federal lockup, was on his way from his cell. Their objective was to grill him for information about the tattoo from Muggs's cellphone.

It was nine p.m. Sunday night and visiting hours had been over for a long time, but Diego's guy—a security guard who just happened to work the weekend night shift—had set them up to see the con.

The clank of the gate release echoed off the concrete floor, and a boy—there was no other way to describe him—walked into the dim, empty visitation room with Diego's pal.

Simon Cooper was about five eight or nine by Eddie's measure. Slim. The orange jumpsuit hung on him. His blond hair was cut short, but some of it still hung down over his forehead. *Puppy*, Eddie thought. Your all-American boy next door. Probably pretty popular with the other cons.

Eddie and Diego stood.

The con sat at the table.

Diego reached out for the guard's extended hand. They shook. Diego stepped back. "Eddie, this is Federico."

Eddie shook the guard's hand. "Fred."

The guard nodded.

"Thanks for setting this up," Eddie said. "We won't forget it."

"*No hay problema*, guys. You got fifteen minutes, tops." He turned and walked to the corner of the room, where he stood, waiting and watching.

Eddie and Diego sat back down.

The boy smiled. Eddie knew the type, a white-collar criminal who could charm the bloomers off Mother Superior.

"Knock it off, kid," he said. "You're cute and all, but it's wasted on us."

The boy seemed just fine with that. He reached over the table and shook their hands respectively. "Simon Cooper. My friends call me Coop. What can I do for you guys?"

Diego pulled a print of the watch tattoo they took off Muggs's phone and slid it across the table.

Coop picked it up and held it face out to them. "Yep, it's mine all right. You like it?"

"It's nice work," Eddie said. "A watch with no hands. Says time is meaningless when you're in the joint. Right, Coop?"

He nodded. "I could do a lot more if I had some decent equipment, you know. Say, you won't mention this to anyone here, will you? I could get a couple of weeks in solitary if they find out I'm slinging ink. It would delay my release."

"We won't say anything."

Coop narrowed his eyes and sat back. "Then what can I do for you?" He fingered the edge of the photo. "You want one like this? I'll give you a good deal."

Eddie laughed. "Thanks, but no tattoos. Here's what we need, Coop."

They brought him up to speed, only including the barest of details. Diego asked, "Any chance you know whose arm this is?"

Coop took another look at it and shook his head. "Sorry."

Eddie and Diego exchanged a look. Total frustration.

Coop went on. "Shouldn't be a problem, though."

They looked back at him.

"I only did eight of those."

Hallelujah, Eddie thought.

Diego was more vocal. "*Gracias a Dios*, we finally caught a break."

"Eight names, Coop? Doesn't sound like it would be too hard for you to provide eight names," Eddie said.

Coop smiled again, showing all his teeth this time. "Don't prematurely ejaculate here, guys. What's in it for me?"

Eddie sighed. Negotiation, always negotiation with cons. "What's on your wish list, kid?"

Coop crossed his arms on top of the table and grinned. "I'm outta here on Tuesday. Free as a bird, sort of. Parole. You know."

Eddie waited for it.

"This was my second go here. First time I did three years. Targeted this fat CEO and managed a half mil in kited checks before they got me. This time, it was eighteen months on a hacking charge."

"Hacking?" Diego asked.

"Yeah. Robin Hood. You know? Hacked the IRS, gave out a bunch of refunds. Didn't take a nickel for myself."

Yeah, I bet, Eddie thought.

"But the Feds didn't seem to care much." Coop looked Eddie straight in the eye. "Point is, I can't come back here."

Eddie said, "Not much I can do about whether you come back here or not."

"Hear me out," Coop said. "The con who watches my back—

literally, if you get my drift—is released next month. He's kept me safe here. Says I remind him of his son. Good old guy. He makes sure I got no problems with lovesick inmates."

Diego snorted. "I can see where that might be a problem for a pretty boy like you. How old are you, anyway? Sixteen?"

The look Coop shot him made him appear altogether different, more like a man who could be taken seriously. "Twenty-three."

Diego said. "Man, you look like a baby, dude."

"Back to your wish list?" Eddie said.

"I need a job, something nice. Something I'm good at. Something mostly indoors."

Eddie nodded. "Yeah? What makes you think I'm the guy to talk to?"

Coop gave him a give-me-a-break look. "I asked around about you when Fred talked to me. I know who you are, Mr. Marino, who you were, what you do. You could use a guy like me."

"I could, eh?"

"Yes, sir. You could. So here's my proposition." He looked Eddie straight in the eye.

Eddie liked this kid more by the minute. *Reminds me of me.*

"I'll help you out with a list of eight names. You check and see who's on the inside and who's on the outside, and maybe one of those outside dudes could be your man. Then—here's the good part—somebody comes around on Tuesday, picks me up and takes me to work at Shea Investigations and Security, where I become a gainfully employed, upstanding member of the community."

Eddie met his direct look. "Sounds like maybe you're getting more bang for your buck outta this deal than we are."

Coop shrugged. "Maybe. You just gotta decide what those names are worth to you." He leaned forward, serious all of a sudden. "I won't let you down, Mr. Marino. I'm good. Ask around. I'll do whatever you need me to do within reason. You won't be sorry."

Eddie spent a long minute looking into Simon Cooper's eyes. The kid didn't look away. What he saw there was reassuring. Earnestness and decency.

He stood. Diego got the signal and stood also.

"Okay, kid," Eddie said. "Give me overnight to talk to a couple of people."

"Meaning your boss, Jordan Welsh?"

Smart kid. "My boss? She's my boss, all right." The boy inched up in Eddie's esteem yet again. "Did your homework, Coop. I'll give you that. Like I said, give me overnight. We'll be in touch."

Chapter 19

∼

"THAT'S NOT HAPPENING." JORDAN spun on her heel and walked away.

Eddie's chin dropped to his chest. He'd come straight to the office Monday morning to plead his case to Jordan. To say she was reluctant was putting it mildly. He couldn't bring Simon Cooper into the firm without Jordan, and he needed Coop's cooperation in the worst way.

Coop might have been right; Jordan might just be the boss after all. "Jordan, hang on a minute. Listen." He hurried after her then realized he wasn't just hurrying, he was scurrying. He slowed down. Only two souls in the entire galaxy could make him scurry. Mama Rose and Jordan. Mama knew it, but he couldn't let Jordan know she had that kind of power over him.

She crossed the reception area to her office, her hands talking as loud as her mouth. Her voice was strident. "Like I don't have enough problems here? I need an ex-con running around the place?"

She strode into her office and slammed the door.

He turned to Gina. "What the hell do I gotta do to get her to give this kid a chance?"

Gina shrugged. "Diamonds are good."

Eddie rolled his eyes. "You're a big help. We need this Cooper guy, and to tell you the truth, I think there's a place around here for a guy like him. But if I'm going to get this by Jordan, I need backup. Who can I get?"

"SIMON COOPER IS A good kid who just got in with the wrong crowd," Ann said.

"Wrong crowd?" Eddie asked. "You mean like the World Wide Web?"

She went on. "I was with the FBI when they made the arrest. That's why my name is on his file. But, Eddie, he's brilliant. There's no end to what he could do with the right guidance. What he needs is a good role model."

Eddie grinned. "I could be a role model."

"Yeah, you're a pillar of virtue, you are." But the look she gave him made him think they might be on the same page. "Simon coming to work for you guys would be good for you, great for him."

"I'd really like to help the kid out, Ann. It seems like the charitable thing to do." He looked up at her, trying for the puppy-dog eyes Simon Cooper had used on him. "I don't think Jordan will go for it, not just on my say-so. If somebody else said it was a good idea, somebody she likes and trusts ...."

Ann narrowed her eyes. "What's your angle, Marino?"

He opened his eyes really wide and said, "Angle? The kid could use some help."

Ann looked skeptical. "What're you up to? There's something in this for you besides Boy Scout of the Year."

He took a minute to consider whether he wanted to come clean to Detective Ann Murphy. The answer was easy. No. She didn't need to know everything. Not now, anyway. Muggs was dead, and Eddie wanted first shot at whoever killed him and took the coins. Ann could just stand in line. But it had been a week and half since the robbery and he was desperate for a break in the case. He needed her to help him convince Jordan.

"Look. Guy I know—guard down at the state pen—calls me up and asks me to do him a large. Says this kid Simon Cooper needs a leg up when he gets out. I owe the guy, so I say, 'Sure, why not?' Like my friend said, and like you said, 'The kid could use some help.' "

"He could." She pursed her lips. "Let's go talk to Jordan."

HE HAD A HELL of a time finding the London Tea Room. Jordan just said it was a half block off Scottsdale Road on First Avenue. She didn't say you had to park in East L.A. to get to it.

The place was located in a standalone house probably built in the late forties or early fifties. He remembered a lot of houses like this one from back in Cleveland—one story, white siding, gabled slate tile roof.

He met Ann at the front door.

She looked at her watch. "Did your watch stop?"

"Where'd you park?"

She turned around. He followed her pointing finger to the curb in front of the place. The Scottsdale PD identification sticker was prominent in the windshield.

"Hell, Ann. I had to walk three blocks."

"Quit bitching. You could have found something closer if you didn't have to take up two parking spaces and put those stupid cones around your Porsche. Honestly, you treat the Porsche like a child."

Eddie grinned. "Porsche. There is no substitute."

They went inside.

Eddie looked around and said to Ann. "You're kidding, right?"

It looked like the Mad Hatter's Tea Party. Not a drop of testosterone in the place. *Chintz curtains with ruffles, stuff on the wall—what are those things? Oh, yeah. Samplers. Embroidered samplers. For crying out loud. What? Did I step back in time to the 1920s?*

Every female from ten to eighty turned to stare when they walked in.

Eddie looked across the room. Jordan and Mama Rose sat at the farthest possible table from the door. And what the hell did they have on their heads?

"Oh, there they are." Ann moved away from him, crossing the room.

"Ann?" There was a brief moment of panic as he realized he was now standing alone and not one of the women had looked away.

He cursed under his breath and began to maneuver around the obstacle course of tiny tables and chairs jammed together like pieces of a jigsaw puzzle with not a single empty seat in the house.

He twisted and turned—chair by chair, table by table. Forty pairs of eyes followed his every move. *I wonder if this is what an exotic dancer feels like at the midnight show.*

Yep. That's what I thought. The tug at his hip pocket confirmed it. He looked down into the smiling face of a young woman with thick eyeglasses and an enormous grin who handed him her business card. "Seriously, lady?"

From a different table he heard, "What is it they say? Biscuits and scones twenty-five dollars … a pot of Earl Grey fifteen dollars … man candy … priceless."

He moved faster, the swish of their whispering followed him all the way to the back of the room.

Jordan glanced up. "There you are."

"Yeah, I barely made it alive. Man-eaters circling out there," he said, looking at her. When did this smoking hot woman start channeling Queen Elizabeth? "That's quite a hat."

Jordan self-consciously slipped off the floppy brimmed lime-green hat and hung it on the corner of her chair. "This is high tea. It's what you wear to high tea."

"Not what *I'd* wear," he said. "Mama, how's your day going?"

Mama Rose reached into a Victoria's Secret bag on the floor

beside her, pulled out a lacy, blue, fluffy thing and waved it at him.

"Something blue," she said. "You know, for the honeymoon."

He gulped. Lingerie. "TMI, Mama."

He leaned down and kissed her on the cheek then pulled out one of the spindly-legged chairs and sat.

Jordan looked at Ann. "What's up? Sounded important when you called me."

Ann laid her hand on Jordan's arm. "I'm calling in a favor. I want you to let Simon Cooper work for you."

Jordan glared at Eddie, then at Ann. "Ganging up on me?"

"Simon who?" Mama asked.

"Simon Says," Jordan said.

"There's this young boy, Mama." Eddie told her the whole shebang.

Mama turned to Jordan. "You should help the poor boy out, sweetie. It's the right thing to do. Pay it forward, honey."

Eddie leaned back in his chair and laced his fingers behind his head. He smiled across the table.

Jordan conceded. "It must be pretty important if you felt like you needed backup." She studied him for a long moment. "Okay. Here are my terms. I want to know everything about this kid. I mean *everything*." She glanced at Mama and winked at Eddie. "You know, boxer shorts, etcetera?"

Eddie glanced at his mother and nodded discreetly.

Jordan went on. "And put Tank on him. We're going to keep such a close eye on Simon Cooper, he won't brush his teeth without someone watching him."

Eddie relaxed. Good. She was on board. "Okay," he said, "but you gotta tell Tank."

Chapter 20

～

THAT AFTERNOON, EDDIE CALLED Diego from his car. "Have your friend Federico get the word to Simon Cooper one of us will be outside the gate tomorrow at noon to pick him up."

"Will do, boss. Must mean Jordan signed the permission slip."

"Smart ass."

"While I got you …." Diego's voice was barely audible above the typical North Scottsdale static. "Guy called me from a pawn shop over by Metro Center. Says he thinks his boss may have some of the Dahlonega coins."

Eddie thought he heard right. "Did you say some of the Dahlonega coins have surfaced?"

"Yeah," he said. Then he broke up again.

"Damn, I can't hear you. Give me a few minutes to get past the hills, Diego. I'll call you back."

Eddie exited the freeway and pulled into the parking lot of the Bowl-a-rama, parking between two school buses.

He keyed in Diego's cell. "Tell me. Who is this guy?"

Two kids, thirteen or so, moseyed out of the bowling alley

past one of the buses and began to circle the Boxster.

Eddie kept an eye on them as Diego began, "He's just some guy who heard we're looking for the museum loot and offering a reward. He says the owner met with someone who had a couple of these odd-looking old coins as samples for potential buyers. Said he's pretty sure they're what we're looking for."

One of the boys was taking an interest in Eddie's custom wheels. He leaned down close—too close. As the kid lifted his hand, Eddie said, "Hang on a sec."

He pushed a button on his key fob and activated the alarm just as the kid's fingers made contact.

The deep robotic voice of the Rattler alarm growled, "Step away from the vehicle."

Both boys jumped back, slammed against the school bus, and ran off into the bowling alley.

Behind his tinted windows, Eddie smiled and went back to Diego. "Text me the info. I'll call Tank, and we'll go down and have a little talk with the nice man."

Metro Pawn was located in a central Phoenix strip mall in a rundown neighborhood west of I-17. The potholes in the parking lot asphalt were so deep it made Eddie glad he'd traded out the Porsche for his Ford Ranger before picking up Tank and heading across town. At one end of the strip mall, three Phoenix PD squad cars and five officers were in the process of shaking down two tough-looking, tattooed kids.

The sign on the pawn shop door read, "Open Twenty-four Hours. We buy and sell it all."

It took a minute for Eddie's eyes to adjust to the darkened, hazy interior. He sniffed a couple of times. What was it about places like this that made them smell like his grandmother's attic?

A woman was behind the counter, her back turned to them. In polite terms, she was plump. If he wasn't feeling polite, she was a pork chop. She turned around. She nodded and leaned on the counter. Her plump face was smooth and would have been pretty if she didn't look like she'd been sucking on a lemon. Her dark hair was long but slicked back off her face and gathered low on her neck into a scrunchie.

"Yeah?" Her voice was low enough that she might have been a four pack a day woman.

"Frank Manheim around?" Eddie asked.

She didn't say anything.

He gave her the look. "Well, is he?"

"She's standing in front of you, Einstein."

"Oh."

"It's Frankie. Not Frank."

"I didn't know. Sorry," Eddie said.

"Yeah, well, guy looks like you doesn't need to have a degree."

"I'm a private investigator. We're working on a case for the Arizona Heritage Museum. Coin collection stolen a little over a week ago. We heard you might know something about it."

"Me? Why?"

"Word on the street is you're shopping a couple of gold coins."

"What street?"

Eddie cleared his throat and settled in for the long haul. "We think they're from the museum."

"What museum?"

He mentally counted to ten. "Like I said, the Arizona Heritage." He tried *the smile*.

"Don't bother, honey. I don't swing your direction."

Tank took over.

"Ma'am, it'd be real nice if you'd help us out just a little. My best friend, guy who was in the war with me, got killed in the robbery."

Eddie couldn't believe it. The old bag melted right in front of him. Her mouth softened, and she was suddenly all dewy-eyed looking at Tank. She came around the counter and pulled his head down onto her chest—Triple Ds, if not more. "Oh, sweetie. I'm so sorry."

Tank peeked out from under her arm and gave Eddie the cheesiest smile he'd ever seen.

Frankie sniffed and stepped back. "Maybe I do know a little something."

She left them and disappeared through a door behind the counter. It was only a minute before she returned with a small, clear acrylic box she laid on the glass top. The lights over the display cases shimmered off the two gold coins inside.

She looked up at Tank. "This what you're looking for, honey?"

Eddie snatched it up before she could stop him. "We'll just take these to the Scottsdale PD. If they don't belong to the collection, you can have them back."

"And if they do?" Frankie asked.

"They're stolen property. This isn't your first time at the rodeo. You know the drill," Eddie said.

Tank gave her a look of sincere apology like it was all Eddie's fault. Eddie narrowed his eyes and sent Tank a signal with a jerk of his head.

Tank picked right up on it and laid his hand on Frankie's arm. "Where'd y'all get 'em, Miss Frankie?"

She turned a cold shoulder on Eddie and smiled at Tank.

What is it about those Southern guys, anyway?

"Got a call from a guy I've handled a few things for. In the past, you know? He says he has these coins, a whole collection. Says if we meet, he'll give me a couple to shop around ..." She paused and seemed to search for the right word, "... to interested collectors. Asked me to meet him at the park. Pretty obvious he wasn't interested in having his picture taken." She looked over her shoulder at the CCTV camera. "So I did." She shrugged.

"You said you've done business with him before?"

Frankie nodded, a look of concern creeping into her eyes.

"And?" Eddie encouraged.

"No names," she said. "I can't tell you who he is."

Eddie glanced at Tank, who smiled and laid a hand on her arm. "It's important, ma'am." He looked up at her with sad eyes.

"I'm sorry, son. This isn't the kind of hardass I want looking for me. No names."

She was scared now, and after what Eddie saw in Tucson, he knew she had good reason to be. Who the hell was this guy?

"Frankie, what does he look like?"

Her eyes flitted between Eddie and Tank. Tank gave her a look of encouragement, and his fingers tightened on her arm.

"Regular, sort of. Gringo. About his height." She lifted her chin toward Eddie. "Maybe a smidge shorter. Dark hair, kinda long. Dark eyes. Would be good looking if he wasn't so scary. The kinda guy who looks at you and you want to go hide under a rock."

Eddie nodded. He knew the type. But it wasn't much help. Could be one of five hundred people, but they had more than yesterday.

He handed her his business card. "This is where you can find me if you decide you want to give him up."

She still looked scared as they turned around and left.

Tank waved back at her. "Bye, y'all."

Out in the parking lot the two men spoke across the hood of Eddie's truck.

"You think Frankie'll be okay?" There was worry in Tank's voice. "Think this creep'll hurt her if he finds out about us?"

Eddie opened the driver's side door. "We'll put somebody over here to keep an eye on her."

JORDAN WAITED ON THE low wall in front of Scottsdale PD Headquarters on Indian School Road. When Eddie and Tank walked up, she stood and met them.

"Can I see it?" she asked.

Eddie pulled the small case with the gold coin from his back pocket and handed it to her. She turned it over in her hands.

An ache started in the pit of her stomach. Someone had killed their friend to get this. She looked up at Eddie.

"Sid Hunter's already in there," she said. "I'm letting you take the lead with the detectives so we don't get our wires crossed."

He nodded. "As far as Ann knows, we are as lost as they are on this case. They don't know about the tattoo and for now, they don't even know about Metro Pawn."

Tank decided to hang around outside while Eddie and Jordan went into the police station.

Detective Ann Murphy and Sid Hunter, the museum curator, waited in one of the interrogation rooms. A jeweler's loupe sat in front of Hunter beside a book titled, *Guide to Rare Coins*.

Eddie laid the acrylic case on the table in front of Sid, who removed the coin and examined it through the loupe. He set it aside for a moment while he opened the book to a marked page, ran his finger over a line of print then looked at the coin again.

"Yes," he said. "These are two of the Type 2 gold dollar coins we had on display, minted 1854 to 1856."

Ann had been leaning forward but relaxed back at his words. "Finally. A break. Metro Pawn Shop, you say?"

Jordan couldn't help but think they'd lost one of their advantages over the cops. More the reason to protect what Simon Cooper could do for them.

Eddie nodded. "Yeah, but this was all owner had, and she didn't know anything about the guy who brought it to her."

Ann looked at him, her eyes distrustful. "Too bad, eh, Eddie?"

"Yes," he said without looking away, "a real shame."

TANK WENT TO BRING the truck around from the parking lot. Eddie and Jordan waited in front of the PD building.

The circles under Eddie's eyes and the hard set of his jaw had Jordan worried. When his eyes met hers, they softened, and he reached out to touch her cheek. He looked tired and stressed.

"We're getting somewhere, finally, right?" she asked.

He was slow to agree, but he did. "We can recover those coins. Frankie was a solid lead. She'll get 'em for us. You should have seen her with Tank. Like a friggin' mother hen."

Jordan laughed. "One other good thing about this."

He looked at her, anxious for good news.

"If he hasn't fenced the coins and he's shopping them around, he's still local."

Eddie's big Ford Ranger rounded the corner. Tank came to a stop and Eddie hopped in.

Jordan leaned back against the wall and dialed Rachel Abromowitz. Finally, some good news to share with the board members. If they played their cards right, Shea Investigations might make it out of this intact after all. A wave of regret washed over her at the thought. Without Muggs, they weren't anywhere close to being intact and wouldn't be for a long time.

Chapter 21

~

IT WAS TUESDAY MORNING—SPRING in Arizona, even in Florence outside the prison. The sky was cerulean, marred by only a few wispy white clouds. Jordan and Diego waited outside the prison gate. The parking lot was uneven, full of crevices and chuckholes with weeds growing up through the asphalt. The Florence State Prison had seen better days for sure. Far from state of the art, it looked like something out of an apocalyptic movie. *Mad Max*, maybe, or *Terminator.* "*Hasta la vista*, baby."

A young blond boy toy strutted toward them.

"Is that him?" Jordan said. "He's cute."

"Yeah, that would be him." Diego got out of the car and walked around.

"Dude," Coop ignored Diego's outstretched hand and pulled him into a hug, "thanks for being my wheels today."

Coop pulled back and turned bright blue eyes and a boyish smile on Jordan. So this was the whiz kid everyone was shouting about. He looked like a schoolboy. Brains. Looks. She could think of a thousand ways to use him at the agency.

"Hello, Coop," she said.

He smiled shyly. "Miss Welsh. Cool. You're really pretty."

She couldn't help herself. She smiled back. "Yeah, yeah, smooth talker. Get in the car."

He hopped into the backseat and leaned forward as Diego got back in. "Sweet ride, dude."

He rubbed his hand along the upholstery of Diego's Wrangler.

"Look, man. You mind if we make one stop before heading to your office?" He rested his elbow on the back of Diego's seat and leaned his chin on his hand. "I'd kinda like to get the prison off me. You know, freshen up? I probably smell like something shoveled out of a barn."

Jordan wrinkled her nose and looked at Diego. "By all means."

Jordan glanced at her watch. "What's taking him so long?"

Coop had been inside the impressive Paradise Valley house where he said his friend lived for over forty-five minutes. Diego and Jordan had opted to wait outside while the boy convict showered and changed clothes.

She looked behind her where Coop's backpack sat, turned and reached for it.

She smiled at him as she unzipped it. "Oops, will you look at what happened? Fell right open."

On top was a folded sheet of paper. She plucked it out and opened it up like it was made of eggshells.

It was exactly what she hoped it would be. "This is it."

Diego leaned across and took a look. "The list of names. All eight of them. Who's …?" he stopped dead.

"Holy shit!" they said in unison.

"Tony …" Jordan said.

"LaSalle," Diego whispered.

They both jumped at Coop's cheerful voice. "See you found the list, okay. Meant to give it to you. Got excited about my," he paused, "shower. You know how it is."

Jordan raised her head, feeling guilty for some reason. "We just …." Her voice trailed off.

He got in the car. "No prob. It's cool. I got nothing to hide from you, boss lady."

"Really? Call me Jordan. Is that your mother?"

A nearly naked woman stood in the open front door, waving at them.

Coop grinned and waved back. "Nope, not Mom," he said. "My friend Veronica."

Diego said, "Veronica, eh? Looks like a nice lady. She bake you some cookies, kid? Is that what took so long?"

"Shame on her." Jordan looked back over the seat. "She's gotta be twice your age."

Coop shrugged. "Age is just a number."

Jordan turned back around. "She tell you that?"

* * *

EDDIE WALKED INTO THE office with Tank.

Gina and Mama Rose were listening to Simon Cooper like he was Deepak Chopra, about to reveal the secrets of the universe. Damn. Gina's eyes were sparkling. Mama Rose looked on dotingly.

Eddie could see already that the boy was going to be trouble.

"Simon. My office. Now." Eddie jerked his thumb back over his shoulder.

Coop looked at Gina and Mama with regret. "Sorry, ladies, guess I'm on the clock." He bowed at the waist and backed away.

For crying out loud. "Simon. Now?"

Tank and Coop followed Eddie into his office. Eddie closed the door behind them and turned to Coop. He was taller than the kid by three or four inches, enough to intimidate.

But the kid didn't seem easily intimidated. "What's up, boss?"

"Enough with the smiles, kid. Save it for somebody who thinks you're cute."

"What did I do now?"

"Gina's off limits to you."

The smile went away. The blue eyes darkened. "Off limits to everybody, or just me? Because I've been inside?"

"Everybody." Eddie got it; he'd been there. This kid seemed to have a past that made him want to challenge anyone who tried to hang a label on him. *Can't blame him.* "Gina's my niece. I look out for her."

Coop smiled. "I get it. She's a beautiful girl. I can see why you'd have to."

Eddie gestured. "This is Tank Sycamore. He's your watchdog, at least until Jordan lets you off leash."

Tank and Coop shook. Tank still looked fairly pissed off at his new assignment. He'd objected in a dozen different ways. None of them had worked.

"Tank," Coop asked. "What's it short for?"

Tank frowned.

Eddie grinned. "Not short for, instead of. It's Beauregard."

Eddie had to hand it to Coop. He didn't blink or even crack a smile—a smart move when you're dealing with a guy whose arms are the size of Tank's. Instead, Coop only said, "Beauregard Sycamore? Must be a Southern family name."

Tank nodded, and with a glare at Eddie, said, "I drove tanks in the army, M1-A1 Abrams."

Coop said, "So it's not because you're built like one?"

"Maybe that too," Tank said.

Coop nodded. "Tank it is."

Eddie said, "Jordan wanted you two to meet up with Steve Keegan down at Bakersfield Labs. They've got results back on the accelerant used in our arson fire case. It was a positive for gasoline. You'll go with him to speak to the owner of the nightclub."

BEHIND THEM, JORDAN OPENED the door.

"Miss Jordan," Tank said, "we're just leaving."

"Tell Steve I said hello," she said.

"Yes, ma'am."

"Thanks, again, Miss Welsh." Coop held the door for Tank then walked out, closing it behind him.

Jordan turned to Eddie and handed him the list from Coop's backpack. "You better sit down."

Eddie opened it, read it, and looked at her. She could have sworn the color drained from his face.

"You saw this." It was a statement, not a question.

She nodded.

He finally followed her advice and sat on the sofa, hard. The list fluttered from his hand. When he looked up at her, it nearly broke her heart.

"LaSalle," he said. "Tony LaSalle." He dropped his head into his hands.

She sat beside him.

He didn't look up. His words were muffled, but she heard every one. "It's personal. It was a personal attack against me. And Muggs. Poor Muggs, he got caught in the crossfire."

"Looks like Mama Rose was mostly right," Jordan said. "It was the mob, or at least someone connected."

"No," Eddie said, "not Vercelli, not his organization. With something like this, Tony had to be acting on his own."

"But why?" Jordan asked.

He didn't answer at first, but when he did, she could see he was as puzzled as she. "Revenge. You know he's never gotten past those years he served in prison. He still blames it on me."

"But, Eddie, this is so—"

"Yeah. It is, isn't it? It does seem excessive. All that trouble, just to get back at me. Why not just come after me? Why plan this whole elaborate scheme?"

Neither of them spoke again for a few minutes, each dealing with the conundrum in their own way.

The dead silence was broken by a knock on the door.

Jordan opened the door and looked up, which was something she seldom had to do. She nearly choked on her surprise.

"Sorry about the bother. I heard your voices, and there doesn't seem to be anyone else about." Palmer Jacoby stood, cap in hand, at Eddie's office door.

Jordan looked around him. Rose and Gina had already left for their lunch date. Tank and Coop had disappeared.

Manners, Jordan. "Palmer. Won't you come in?"

His long legs carried him into the room. For a guy so tall, he moved with a kind of grace and economy.

His gaze found Eddie still sitting on the sofa. "Marino," he said. "Have I come at a bad time?"

Eddie stood and seemed to shake off the despair sitting on him just moments before. "Palmer, my man." He shook hands with the lanky thief. "Good to see you again. What can I do ya for? Have a seat."

Palmer shook his head. "No, thank you. Won't take more than a minute of your time. I have a plane to catch. There's an opportunity in Shanghai I believe I'd like to look into. After I tell you what I've come to say, I think it's wise for me to make myself scarce a while."

Eddie leaned back against the edge of his desk. Jordan went to stand beside him.

Palmer began. "I've been at my craft for nigh onto thirty years, and was ever so careful no one was ever hurt in any of my endeavors. That our mutual friend was killed at the museum is eating at my very core. My conscience won't abide my silence any longer. I'll give you the name of the man who first contacted then hired me to disable the museum system."

He waited a long beat then said, "It was Tony LaSalle."

Eddie stood away from the desk, went to Jacoby, took his hand and shook it gratefully. "Thank you, Palmer. I know this wasn't easy for you."

Palmer nodded and turned his cap around in his hands. He wouldn't look at either of them. "No. Not easy at all. Mr. LaSalle's reputation for violence is well known. I thought a good while before deciding to come to you." He turned away. "Best be on my way."

Jordan walked out with him and opened the lobby door. Before he went out, she laid her hand on his arm. "Eddie told me the code of silence is paramount in your line of work. What you've done today is a good thing. We'll find LaSalle and take care of him."

He looked down at her. Not all men could. "I hope so. I enjoy living here."

Chapter 22

~

Mary Welsh would curl up and die if she knew Anthony Vercelli, crime lord—for want of a better title—lived less than a mile from her in the opulent community of Troon in North Scottsdale. Vercelli wasn't exactly the friendly neighbor you'd borrow a cup of sugar from.

Jordan had only been to Vercelli's place once about six months earlier, when she and Eddie were investigating the embezzlement of funds from the Moon & Stars Foundation. That was where and when she'd first encountered Tony LaSalle.

Eddie's history with Anthony Vercelli was long, dark, and complicated. Vercelli took Eddie off the streets when he was a young boy and *employed* him. Eddie ran errands for Vercelli and his businesses, most of which were illegal in one way or another. After Eddie came back from a stint in the Army where he learned hi-tech security and encoding techniques, Vercelli hired him once again. A move of Vercelli's main operations to Arizona brought Eddie Marino to the southwest. The two came to a parting of the ways, and Eddie went out on his own. To the best of Jordan's knowledge, he never looked back. She'd been scared and insecure when Eddie had told her about his past, and she had to admit that at times it affected the way she looked at him.

Tony LaSalle was basically a henchman for Vercelli. From the first, it had been obvious LaSalle hated even the thought of Eddie Marino, a sentiment he evidently had acted on when he robbed the museum and killed Muggs. Why he chose this moment and method to exact his revenge was still a mystery.

Vercelli was out back, improving his short game on his private putting green. The view from his patio took Jordan's breath away. His Tuscan-style estate sat high enough on the side of a hill to offer a vista of the entire Valley of the Sun. His vanishing edge pool disappeared over the side of the yard and dropped off straight into a lush landscape of saguaro cacti and sage.

Dressed in Bermuda shorts and a Ralph Lauren golf shirt, Vercelli didn't look like a man who could terminate someone's very existence with a snap of his fingers. But Jordan knew that close up, his black eyes revealed the soul of a vicious, cunning predator.

He looked up as the two descended the flagstone steps. "*Eduardo*. Jordan. I was just thinking about you two the other day. What would you say if I told you I might hire your firm to investigate this problem I seem to be having with the Mexican drug cartel?"

Cartel? Jordan caught her breath. This couldn't be a coincidence. She looked at Eddie, who at least made a pretense of taking it all in stride. "Since when do you have business with the Mexican cartel?" he asked.

"Since never," Vercelli said. "They seem to want a piece of my ass lately. I have no idea why. Anyway, this is a pleasant surprise. I don't see you nearly often enough."

Eddie's tone grew serious. "You won't think it's so pleasant when I tell you why we're here."

Vercelli motioned to his Man Friday, who took his putter. The three of them moved to a spacious terrace, where they seated themselves on a rattan sectional around a copper-based table.

"Leon, rustle us up some refreshment."

Leon, the Man Friday *du jour*, didn't meet Mary Welsh's standards of a prim and proper butler. He was about six feet six, with arms the size of telephone poles. The butt of his handgun stuck out of the shoulder holster he wore over his Gold's Gym tank. "Right away, Mr. V."

Jordan watched him leave, his muscular buttocks rolling in his gym shorts like two bowling balls.

Vercelli laid his hand on Eddie's shoulder. "I was truly sorry to hear about what happened to Muggs. He was a good boy."

"Muggs is why I'm here."

Vercelli crossed his ankle over his knee, leaned back and waited.

Eddie took a deep breath. "I came for Tony."

"Tony?" Vercelli asked.

Jordan's heartbeat kicked up, for a very specific reason. Anthony Vercelli frowned. Not a good sign.

"It was LaSalle who hit the Arizona Heritage Museum," Eddie said. "He killed my friend. He killed Muggs."

Vercelli didn't say anything at first. He just sat quietly while Leon set a silver tray on the table with a pitcher of Mojitos, three Tom Collins glasses, and a platter of fully loaded nachos. He was as bad as the Abromowitz sisters.

Vercelli leaned over, filled one of the glasses, and offered it to her.

She shook her head and pointed to her watch. "Thank you. Not now. It's a little early for me." Jordan could not see herself sharing a drink with this man, regardless of the fact that he had helped Eddie and his family out.

"So, *Eduardo*, I know you're not the kind of man to make empty accusations. I'm assuming you have proof of this transgression."

Eddie nodded. "You're right. I don't make empty accusations."

"So you've come to me why?" Vercelli asked. The keen look in his eye said he knew exactly why.

"Permission, sir," Eddie said. "Out of respect, to ask your permission to go after LaSalle."

Vercelli's voice was considerate, even benign. "As far as I know, after you left and he took over your position, Tony's been a true and loyal employee." Vercelli went on. "I know there's bad blood between you two, but bad blood can be overcome."

Eddie said, "Up until now there was no bad blood on my part. But Tony, he holds a grudge. You know he does."

Vercelli nodded. "He did you a large favor, son. Spent three years in lock-up on your behalf."

"With respect. He spent three years in lock-up on *your* behalf."

Vercelli's jaw tightened.

Jordan didn't know all the details, but she knew enough. When Eddie worked for Vercelli he was asked to do something so dark Eddie not only refused to do the job, he left the organization. Tony LaSalle had no such qualms. He did the job and took the fall. In her eyes, LaSalle was worse than Vercelli. He was a coiled viper ready to strike. The only time she'd seen LaSalle, she'd noted the hatred that spewed from him when he looked at Eddie Marino.

Had he robbed the museum for monetary gain, revenge, or something else? Even Eddie admitted he didn't have a clue. One thing was certain. It was Eddie who LaSalle targeted that night. Muggs took Eddie's place at the last minute and paid for it with his life.

"I can't give you my permission." Vercelli's voice was low and even. "My employees' actions are my responsibility. I'll bring him in."

"It's personal," Eddie said.

"I know. I don't care. Don't go against me on this, *Eduardo*. If you find him before we do, bring him to me. Let me weigh the evidence; then I'll be the one to decide what to do."

"We have enough history for you to know I can't do that. Won't."

Vercelli stood. His eyes went flat. He clamped down so hard a muscle jerked in his jaw.

Jordan could barely breathe.

"There will be consequences." Vercelli's eyes shifted to Jordan.

Eddie stood, blocking Vercelli's line of sight. "What I do, I own. Me. Nobody else."

Eddie was so mad when he walked out the front door he was shaking.

Jordan was thinking now would be a good time for one of those Mojitos.

She couldn't believe Eddie had just stood nose to nose with Anthony Vercelli and defied his will. She didn't even want to think what that might mean. The theme song to *The Godfather* ran through her head, and she worried about receiving an offer they couldn't refuse.

"LaSalle! You piece of shit!" Eddie shouted and broke into a run.

Her head jerked up.

Tony LaSalle ran down the cobbled driveway toward a silver Lexus sedan.

Jordan's thought echoed Eddie's. *Piece of shit!*

Eddie cut across the yard, hurdling a row of low oleander bushes. LaSalle made it to the car and jumped in.

Jordan grabbed Eddie's spare keys from her bag and ran for Eddie's truck, hitting the remote starter on the fly. She got in behind the wheel and threw it in gear.

The Lexus's tires squealed and smoked as LaSalle careened down the driveway. Eddie ran out in front of it.

Eddie, you'll get yourself killed. She stomped on the accelerator in a move to block LaSalle's escape.

A grocery delivery truck pulled into the driveway square in front of Eddie's Ford Ranger. The startled deliveryman looked through his windshield and threw up his hands. She slammed into reverse and screamed backward into the street.

The Lexus jerked to a stop before lurching straight at Eddie.

LaSalle was trying to kill him.

Eddie spun to the side, but LaSalle clipped him with the right front fender as he swung the Lexus around.

Jordan gripped the wheel. "Oh, Jesus. Eddie!"

Eddie hit the pavement and tumbled all the way down the incline.

As the Lexus pulled onto the street, Jordan headed straight for him. "Wanna play chicken?"

The Lexus skidded around Eddie's truck and sped away. Jordan stomped on the brakes.

Eddie sprang to his feet, ran to the truck, threw open the door, and jumped in.

"Oh my God. Are you okay?"

Eddie pounded the seat beside him. "Go. Just go."

Jordan spun the wheel, floored it, and took out a creosote bush as she hopped the curb then straightened out and fishtailed down the street.

The Lexus was already out of sight when they made the turn for the entry gates. The gate was on its way back down. Jordan never let up, but turned her head and looked away as she sped through. The gate came down, missing the truck by inches.

They slammed to a stop at the main turn-off onto Dynamite Road.

The Lexus was disappearing fast.

"Right!" Eddie yelled. "Go right!"

She did, barreling down Dynamite Road like a bat out of hell, but the truck was big and heavy. The Lexus was light, and its big engine nearly let it take flight.

Pedal to the floor, but she wasn't gaining at all.

She slowed but didn't stop at the red light and nearly put the truck on two wheels careening left onto Pima. She kicked it up to seventy-five in the fifty mile per hour speed zone and prayed no cops were around.

By the time they hit Happy Valley Road, it was obvious they'd lost him. He could have turned off into any one of several residential neighborhoods and gotten lost in the maze of streets. She pulled into a parking lot at Pinnacle Peak and Pima and shut off the truck.

She sat back and looked at Eddie.

"Goddammit." Eddie smashed his fist against the dash.

Tony LaSalle was in the wind.

Eddie looked at her, dead serious. "The Mexican cartel's after Vercelli? This means Tony LaSalle is somehow in bed with them."

Chapter 23

～

TONY LaSALLE LIVED IN the Arcadia area of Central Phoenix. Jordan didn't know how Eddie came by this knowledge. She didn't ask him about it, because in Eddie's world it made sense to keep track of both your friends and your enemies, and besides, the poor guy had a lot on his mind. If they were going to recover the Dahlonega coins and get the goods on Tony LaSalle for killing Muggs, Eddie had to be on top of his game.

The '70s ranch-style house was on a side street in the Arcadia district south and east of prestigious Fashion Square. It was a long, low masonry house with a shake shingle roof. An extensive well-groomed lawn stretched out in front of it, and two huge acacia trees shaded the house. It looked like the occupant should be a geriatric Republican, not the hired gun of one of the country's most notorious crime syndicates.

"Not what you expected?" Eddie asked.

She gave him a small smile and shook her head. "Not exactly."

"Then you'd probably be interested in knowing the neighbors to the north are a couple in their eighties, to the south a retired game show host in his nineties. More the standard Arcadia profile?"

"And in the middle, a stone cold killer." She paused. "Nice neighborhood."

They circled the block, looking for signs that he might have parked down the street and walked home. But they didn't see anything.

They parked the truck in the alley and went through the backyard gate at Tony's place.

The locks and alarm system didn't even slow down Eddie Marino, whose training as security and intelligence in the Army served Shea Investigations handsomely these days.

They shut the kitchen door behind them and waited, listening. There were no sounds except the ticking of a grandfather clock down the hallway.

The kitchen needed serious remodeling. Colorful Mexican tiles covered the countertops. Walnut cabinets and appliances with black glass fronts also dated the place. It was cleaner than clean. If any cooking had gone on in the funky kitchen, it was years ago. The only signs of human activity were a two-slot stainless-steel toaster in one corner and a high-end espresso machine. She looked around, shaking her head. Tony LaSalle was a stick of dynamite waiting to blow, yet his house was positively cozy. What was that about?

They walked into a living room dominated by big, overstuffed furniture. Sun streamed in through a sparkling clean picture window looking out on the street.

A photograph on the mantle shelf stopped the sweep of her gaze. A woman in her late twenties and a young girl of about four or five smiled into the sun from a swing set.

Eddie came back up the hallway. "No sign of him here, but I found these in the trash can in the bathroom."

She cocked her head and waited.

"Brochures from the Arizona Heritage Museum detailing the exhibit of the Dahlonega coin collection."

"Well, that validates it for me," Jordan said. She turned back to the photo. What she didn't know about Tony LaSalle would fill a stadium, including, "He has a little girl? Is this his wife?"

Eddie squinted from across the room. "It's his sister and her kid."

She nodded.

He looked around. "There's nothing here. Let's go."

They went back outside to Eddie's truck. He called Tank and put him on speaker. "How's our child?"

Tank laughed. "He's a good little boy."

Jordan could just imagine him patting Coop on the head. "Maybe you can take him to the gun range tonight?" she asked.

Tank sighed. "Guess I could. Do I get overtime, boss?"

Jordan said, "In your dreams. He needs to be trained."

Eddie said, "LaSalle's on the run. We gotta figure out who'd hide him. Think you two are up to it?"

In the background, she heard Coop say, "Coolness. A caper."

Tank's reply was desert riverbed dry. "Take it easy, kid."

METRO PAWN WAS OPEN for business.

A geeky young guy in a white-collared shirt under an ASU sweatshirt sat behind the counter reading the Steve Jobs autobiography. He looked up as Jordan and Eddie walked in.

"Something I can do for you?" he asked.

"Frankie," Eddie said.

The young man jerked his head toward the back room. "Is she expecting you? She's entertaining."

"She knows us." Eddie didn't stop, heading toward the back room like he owned the place.

Jordan followed, her head swiveling as item after item came into view, each more bizarre than the one they'd just passed by—a Nazi helmet with the business end of a bayonet sticking out the front, an old-fashioned wooden dynamite detonator like those used back when the railroads were first built, a set of gold-capped false teeth. She had a second look at those.

Eddie led her straight to the back room, where Diego sat in an armchair in front of a big screen watching *Telemundo*, one of those boom-chicky-boom variety shows.

A table beside him bore several plates of cupcakes, brownies, chocolate-iced doughnuts, and Moon Pies. Diego's face was smeared with chocolate icing.

"Better watch it, dude. You'll eat so much you won't fit in your Jeep anymore," Eddie said.

Diego looked up, his expression sheepish.

He took his feet off the hassock and sat up straight. "Boss. Jordan."

A heavy-set woman came through a side doorway, carrying a tray with a tall glass full of ice and a bottle of IB root beer.

She smiled at Eddie and puffed a few strands of escaped hair off her face. "Eddie, nice to see you."

Eddie made introductions. "Frankie Manheim. Jordan Welsh, my partner."

Frankie set the tray by Diego, who seemed to be trying to pretend the sugar explosion sitting beside him was for someone else.

Frankie turned to Eddie. "I really want to say thanks for sending Diego here to watch over me. Makes me feel as well-guarded as the Crown Jewels. And he's not so bad to look at either." She smiled down at Diego. "You need anything, sweetie?"

"Good to hear," Eddie said. "Frankie, have you seen or heard from Tony LaSalle?"

Frankie's mouth fell open. She stared at him.

Eddie nodded. "We know it was him, Frankie. So, if he comes around—"

She straightened up and thrust out her chin. "You think he's coming back here, don't you?"

"I think he might," Eddie admitted.

"You put me in danger, Mr. Marino. Made me a target. Next thing you know there'll be cops all over the place, and LaSalle's going to think I narced him out."

"Diego's here. Nobody's going to hurt you, Frankie. And there won't be any cops around. They don't know it was Tony who pulled the job, and we're not going to tell them just yet."

The young boy from the front room stood in the doorway. "Frankie, couple of people outside to see you. Say they're cops."

If looks were bullets, Eddie would be shot through the heart. "I friggin' told you. Didn't I?" Frankie huffed.

Jordan tried to smooth things over. "They're just here to ask you some questions about the coins. Don't worry."

Detectives Neil Thompson and Ann Murphy came to the doorway.

When Ann saw Eddie and Jordan, she said, "Impeding our investigation again, guys?"

Eddie and Jordan looked at each other.

"You need to get out of our way," Thompson said. "This is police work."

"Get out of your way?" Eddie was hot. "You wouldn't have jack if it wasn't for us. And you know it."

"Think much of yourself, Marino? You're not that good." Neil drew back his shoulders and thrust out his chin.

"Yes," Eddie shrugged, "I most certainly am."

Jordan went to Ann and took hold of her arm. "Let's step outside. Something I want to tell you."

OUTSIDE ON THE SIDEWALK, Jordan said in a low voice, "Ann, we know who it is."

"And you're going to share this information with me, right?"

Yes. She was going to share it with Ann. If Eddie knew, he'd be livid. She wasn't sure he'd ever forgive her, but now that she knew who they were after, she was more than a little afraid. Having the police looking for Tony at the same time they were sounded like a good idea. If the cops could get to LaSalle first, it would be better for everyone—certainly safer for Eddie. LaSalle would pay for Muggs, and Eddie wouldn't go to jail for killing LaSalle.

"It's a guy named Tony LaSalle. He works for Anthony Vercelli as—"

Ann sighed. "I know who Tony LaSalle is. What makes you think it's him?"

"We just know. We have ways of getting to things that would make your hair curl. Don't ask."

"Jordan, you and Eddie have never steered me wrong, but without evidence, there's nothing I can do."

"We'll get it for you, but Eddie can't know I gave you the name."

Ann looked at her, understanding in her eyes. "Okay. In the meantime, I guess I could say we heard from an anonymous source about LaSalle. I could list him as a person of interest." Ann took out her notebook and wrote in it.

"Thanks, Ann."

IT TOOK FORTY-FIVE MINUTES to heat Jordan's spa. Eddie and Jordan sat at the kitchen table and drank red wine while they polished off the lasagna her housekeeper Hannah had cooked the night before.

Once the bubbles were going and the two were naked in the spa, the heat and wine had relaxed their inhibitions enough to open them up to experimentation. There were actually a couple of times Jordan worried Eddie might drown.

When they got out, all loose and lovey-dovey, and went inside, Eddie nearly spoiled it all by asking, "So what did you talk to Ann about today?"

She couldn't tell him the truth. He couldn't know, at least not now, that she had given LaSalle up to the police.

"You know," she said, "I was just trying to get her out of your hair. Told her Diego was on Frankie. Told her we'd been making a little headway, but nothing major. She said to talk to her again when we have some hard evidence." *Only half a lie.*

The idea of cappuccino and Netflix under the covers sounded like a swell idea. Jordan went to turn on the steam shower while Eddie put on his jeans and went into the kitchen to start up Jordan's whiz-bang cappuccino maker. She joined him in the kitchen.

"Popcorn?"

"Make a double helping," he said. "I have a healthy appetite tonight."

Eddie always had a healthy appetite, and not just for food.

Her phone rang while she was still tending the popper.

"Fire" by the Ohio Players. It was Keegan. "Hey, Steve." She cradled the phone under her chin and turned the popcorn off.

"I called to let you know we closed the case on The Jokers Wild," he said. "Got a couple of clean prints off a cigarette lighter found at the scene. It took a while to identify them because of the damage caused by the extreme heat. Turns out the guy had a record—professional arsonist who already served two stretches for different fires. We brought him in. Phoenix PD leaned on him and promised him a deal if he gave up his paycheck. It was the club owner."

"Congratulations to us all," Jordan said. "You're the man, Steve."

The arson case was closed. The police were now looking for Tony LaSalle. Jordan felt really good for the first time in two weeks, so good in fact she let Eddie choose the movie. Make that movies; he'd opted for an *Expendables* marathon.

Chapter 24

~

IT WAS THURSDAY NOON. As always, Kierland Commons in North Scottsdale was a little bit of Beverly Hills—high fashion, upscale restaurants, all the bells and whistles. Mary Welsh and her American Express card nearly lived there or down the road at Fashion Square.

One of her favorite lunch places was *Café du Mer*. The ambiance, obsequious service, and delicate cuisine were right up her alley after many, many evenings spent with the robust flavors of Welsh's Steak and Chophouse.

The interior was red, black, and white—everywhere. The servers wore stiff white shirts with red ties and aprons and black stovepipe pants. There were a lot of personal greetings, and her favorite cocktail always waited at her special table.

She sipped it now; nothing like a Grey Goose martini with extra olives to start off a good meal. She liked them dry, so dry that she instructed the bartender, "Don't add the vermouth. Just walk by it with the vodka."

She was still working on her first but beginning to think about her second when Rose Marino appeared in the entryway, her head swiveling.

Mary stood and waved. "Rose! Rose, dear. Over here."

Rose hugged Mary then sat. The waiter appeared at her side, picked up her napkin, snapped it smartly and attempted to lay it in her lap. Rose grabbed his wrist and glared at him like he was some kind of pervert. "Give it a rest, sonny. I'll take care of the lap work."

Mary sent him away with a wave.

Mary laid her hand atop Rose's. "I'm so glad to see you, darling. This was a brilliant idea. I have to say I'm most flattered to be asked to help you pick out your trousseau."

Rose's smile was huge. "I'm just happy as a clam you agreed to do it. I never told you this, but you're my fashion role model, Mary. Always so put together and chic. I want to look pretty for Mark on our honeymoon. Thank you for agreeing to help me shop."

The two women chatted. When it came time to order, Rose complained, "I don't know what to get. Nothing's in English."

Mary was delighted to do the honors. "Don't worry, Rose dear. I'm an expert at French cuisine, and nearly everything else as well." She laughed, only half-joking. "But you wouldn't know I had a single brain cell if you asked my children."

Rose snagged a breadstick from the glass vase on the table and munched. "Don't I know it? Rotten kids."

When the food came, Rose looked at her plate and said it was all too pretty to eat, but eat she did, every bite.

When they finished and went outside into the bright Arizona sun, Mary rubbed her hands together enthusiastically and said, "Where to start? I have it. Lingerie. Let's go. The timing's perfect. Everyone's eating lunch. The stores won't be busy."

AND SO IT WAS—LINGERIE then swimsuits. Rose purchased a scandalous purple bra with plenty of padding and a turquoise swimsuit with a pretty little skirt around the middle.

Pleased with their purchases, they stood on the corner about to cross the street to a dress shop specializing in resort attire when a black Expedition barreled around the corner and screeched to a halt in front of them. The passenger door swung open, and a man jumped out. He was lean with long black hair. Mary noticed his clothes. Urban chic was the way she'd have described them. Expensive jeans, designer T-shirt.

The thought crossed Mary's mind that he was sexy in a dark, bad boy sort of way. She didn't have time for second thoughts as he took hold of the handle on the back door and yanked it open. He grabbed Rose by the arm and pulled her.

"What!" Mary didn't think twice. Shopping bags flew everywhere as she jumped on his back and began to beat him on the head with her Prada clutch. "Run, Rosie, run! Leave her the hell alone, you brute."

He jerked his elbow, smashing her face as she hung over his shoulder. Her head snapped back. Stars swam, and she fell onto the cushion of the shopping bags then rolled over onto the sidewalk.

Rose screamed like a banshee. He shoved her into the backseat, slammed the door, and jumped in.

Agitated people came from the stores and cafés nearby and stared as the tires spun, grabbed, and the car sped away. One man even ran out into the roadway after it, but stopped as the Expedition pulled out onto Scottsdale Road.

A hand came into Mary's line of sight. She took it and was pulled to her feet by one of the young parking valets. "Are you okay, ma'am?"

She patted her hair and pulled down her pastel blue skirt, noticing the red stain at the hemline. "Oh, damn! My favorite Chanel." She examined her bloody knee. "And that's going to be a scab."

He gathered up Rose's shopping bags as Mary tried to figure out what had just happened. Was Rose really kidnapped? Were the kids playing a trick? She was confused and scared, and suddenly she felt very, very old. She made her way to a bench and sat. The valet set the bags at her feet.

Jordan's number was the first on her favorites list. She spoke into the phone. "Call Jordie."

IT WAS NEARLY ELEVEN Thursday night, and the mood at the office was tense, somber. No word had come in as to the whereabouts of Rose. Eddie could only remember being so terrified twice before—once when he'd been told his father was dead and again last year when Jordan had nearly died in a car bomb incident while working the Moon & Stars Foundation case. Neither had made him feel as helpless as he did now.

He leaned against the sofa cushions as Jordan walked back into his office, shaking her head.

"Where's he taken her?" He looked up. "Why would Tony take Mama when it's me he wants?"

Jordan leaned over him and cradled his head. "We'll find Mama Rose. We will."

"Sorry," Coop said, his voice soft and apologetic. He stood in the open doorway. "I got something, you guys."

THE THREE WENT INTO the back room where the state-of-the-art video surveillance equipment had been upgraded even more and rearranged by Simon Cooper earlier in the day when they first got word Rose had been taken. There were so many flashing screens and scanners, buttons and switches, it looked like the operations control center at the Pentagon.

Coop took a seat at the panel and started a video. "I hacked the security system for the shopping area."

"You go, Coop." Jordan offered her fist for a bump.

As the screen came to life, Mama Rose and Jordan's mother stood on the corner, waiting to cross. They chatted. Mary laid her hand on Rose's arm while Rose threw back her head and laughed. The big black vehicle roared around the corner, and Rose was gone in a flash.

It was all there, the whole incident, and it validated what Mary had told them about the vile, evil man who took Eddie's mama. They knew it was Tony LaSalle, but knowing it didn't put them any closer to getting her back or learning what he wanted.

Eddie watched the video, eyes suspiciously bright. "My little mama put up a damn good fight. And Mary was no slouch either. How's she doing?"

Jordan shrugged. "Skinned knee, black eye. But she's not complaining, if you can believe it. She's scared and waiting to hear, just like the rest of us."

Eddie's phone rang. He looked at the screen. "The number's blocked."

Jordan held her breath.

"Eddie Marino." His voice shook. "Tony. You touch her and you're—"

Jordan squeezed his arm and shook her head. He took a deep breath, let it out and switched over to speaker.

Tony's hateful voice was amused. "I'm what, Marino? What were you going to say?"

Eddie nearly choked but kept his cool. "What's the deal? Just tell me and let's get this over with."

From somewhere behind Tony, Mama's high-pitched, muffled voice delivered ultimatums worthy of a street thug. "You better let me go if you know what's good for you, punk."

"It's not your mom I want, Marino—not like you didn't know."

Rose shrieked. "My son Eddie will nail your knees to the floor, slime ball!"

Coop looked at Jordan. His mouth hung open in amazement and he whispered, "Slime ball? She'll get herself killed if she doesn't stop."

Tony went on, his voice away from the phone, "Shut it, bitch!" Then back. "Your old lady has a mouth on her. Here're my terms. I'll let her go, safe and sound, not a single hair on her old gray head ruffled. But you're going to take her place."

"Why?" Eddie said. "Why you doing this? Why now?"

No response.

Eddie looked at Jordan. "Tell me when and where you want me. I'll do whatever you say as long as I see she's safe."

Feelings spun inside Jordan like a whirlwind. Mama was safe. *Relief.* But Tony wanted Eddie. *Fear.* And Eddie was going. There was nothing she could do about it. Above all else, she felt *powerless.*

Eddie disconnected the call, stood and headed to the front of the office. She followed, hearing the plea in her voice. "Let's get the guys in place before you do this. *Please.* Call in Tank and Diego off the street. I can call Ann. Let's do it the right way."

He never turned around or looked at her. She knew there would be no reasoning with him when she heard his voice. It was dead flat. "No. No one else. Just me. It's all me this time."

PAPAGO PARK IN SOUTH central Phoenix was popular with families and hikers. Situated very near the impressive Phoenix Zoo, it was a desert area where the hiking trails and climbing areas brought people from all over the valley. The beauty of the red rock formations was the big draw.

At night, it was a whole different matter—isolated, dark, and quiet. And it was Tony LaSalle's choice of exchange points.

Jordan and Eddie waited in Jordan's Pilot under a halogen light pole in the deserted parking area at the base of one of the main trailheads.

They held hands but were both so keyed up and paranoid, conversation was limited.

"What's your plan?" Something about the atmosphere and the situation made her whisper.

He didn't speak for a minute. "The plan is to go with him quietly, no resistance. When you and Mama are safely away, then …." He looked at her in the darkened interior of the car, the dash lights casting his face half in shadow, half in light. "I'll know what move to make when the time comes."

"Why's he doing this? What does he want?"

She could see by his face, he had no more idea than she. "You're just going to let him take you? Not put up a fight? Eddie? No! I can't stand by and let you just walk right into it. No!"

He squeezed her hand.

"LaSalle's a killer." She was barely able to speak.

He looked at her sideways and shrugged.

"Yes," she went on. "I know. You can take better care of yourself than ninety-nine percent of the rest of humanity, but Eddie, this scares me. LaSalle scares me, not to mention we might be dealing with the cartels."

"Look, babe. This is me. This is what I do, what I was trained for, and yeah, I'm better at it than anyone else, even better than Tony LaSalle. You gotta promise me you won't come after me. This guy's deadly. He'd just as soon shoot you as look at you, and if he takes you, it's just one more thing he can use against me."

She looked at him, and while she knew he was right, the words still came hard. "Okay. I won't try anything on my own." *But I never said I wouldn't come with backup.* Half a promise, half a lie. He did that sleight of hand with her all the time. *Presto-chango.*

He looked in her eyes. "I mean it this time."

She prayed he wouldn't see her deception.

"Trust me," he said. "I'll be fine."

"I know," she said. And he would be, because she'd see to it.

Chapter 25

∽

THE ARRANGED TIME CAME and went, and still they sat in the car. The temperature dropped in the early morning hours. Jordan reached into the backseat for a lightweight jacket, shrugged into it, and slipped her hip holster outside it. No matter what Eddie said, if things went bad, she wanted to be ready for trouble.

In her whole life if she'd ever seen anyone who looked untrustworthy, it was Tony LaSalle.

"Eddie."

Headlights appeared along the access road to the parking lot, moving slowly.

She pulled her hand out of his and instinctively reached for her gun. He stayed her hand.

It was the black Expedition from the video. She could hear her heartbeat in her ears.

The car pulled up to the entrance of the parking lot and stopped. It just sat there, and she couldn't take it.

"What is he doing?" she asked.

"Waiting. Making sure there's nobody else around." How could Eddie's voice be so steady?

When nothing else seemed to be happening and she thought she'd have to scream out loud, Eddie opened his car door and stepped out into the night.

She hit auto-dial on her phone, laid it on the seat, opened the driver's door, and got out too.

He looked at her. "Stay cool."

She nodded, anything but cool.

The Expedition pulled forward and stopped again about fifteen yards away into the circle of light beneath the light pole. The passenger door opened, and Tony LaSalle stepped out.

He stood still for a long moment, looking into the desert surrounding the parking lot. His voice wasn't loud, but it carried in the night air. "Anybody else out there, Marino?"

"You know me, Tony. Mr. Congeniality. You said come alone. I came alone."

"Right. Mr. Congeniality." He looked around again, opened the back door and pulled Mama Rose out beside him. She stumbled but he didn't let her fall.

Eddie walked around to the front of the car and looked back at Jordan. She joined him. His whole body was vibrating. It was her turn to steady him.

Tony said something Jordan couldn't hear. The driver's door opened, and another man stepped out of the Expedition. Light bounced off the top of his head—longish curly black hair. His face was in shadow. His right arm hung loosely at his side, the unmistakable silhouette of a military-style automatic pistol visible in the dim light.

Jordan's breath came fast and shallow. She reached for her holster, but Eddie whispered, "No. They're just being careful. He wants me alive for some reason, and he won't shoot you right now. It would be against his twisted code of ethics."

Tony had a grip on Mama Rose's upper arm. He began to pull her along with him. "Let's go, old girl."

Mama Rose shrieked, "Don't touch me, goomba. I can walk on my own."

The two drew closer. Eddie nodded at Jordan, and they began to walk side by side toward Tony and Mama Rose. Closer. Closer still.

Mama's hands were bound in zip ties, but that didn't keep her from jerking them upward and trying to pop Tony in the nose. "Run, Eddie, I got this."

"Jesus, lady. Knock it off, will ya?"

He stopped walking about ten feet from Jordan and Eddie. They stopped too.

"You okay, Mama?" The smile on Eddie's face was heart breaking. "I want you to go with Jordan."

Rose began to cry. "No, Eddie. He'll hurt you."

"It's okay, Mama. He just wants to talk." His eyes lifted. "Isn't that right, Tony?"

"Yeah," the very definition of sarcasm, "talk, and you're the one who's gonna be doing the talking."

"Me?" Eddie's expression was confused.

Tony shoved Mama, and she stumbled. Jordan lurched forward and caught her.

"Go, Jordan." Eddie didn't look away from Tony or the other guy for a second. "Take Mama and go."

"Mama, get in the back." She couldn't keep her voice from shaking.

"Jordan, don't leave him." Mama's voice shook too.

"I promised." There wasn't anything else to say. She shut the door behind Mama Rose, got behind the wheel, started the car, and drove from the parking lot out onto the city streets.

It nearly killed her.

She only looked back once. Tony's man had moved to within a few feet of Eddie and aimed his gun at Eddie's chest. Tony grabbed the front of Eddie's shirt with one hand and clocked him in the face with the other. Jordan looked away. There would be more, and she wasn't in a position to stop it. Not yet.

She could barely speak, but managed. "I got her. Go."

Tank's voice came back over the phone speaker. "Roger that."

Jordan pushed the accelerator and turned onto McDowell Road. Behind her, Mama sobbed.

"He'll be okay, Mama. We'll get him back."

"How could you just leave him there?"

"I couldn't help it. He made me promise. I'm taking you to Eddie's place. Mark's there, waiting for you. Coop will be inside with the two of you, and a couple of hard cases will be on the door. Tank and Diego are already on it, Mama. They'll get him back. You heard, right?"

But Mama Rose just cried harder. "My Eddie."

BY THE TIME JORDAN delivered Mama Rose to Eddie's place in Kierland, Jordan had cut the zip ties. The old girl was quivering like a bowl of Jell-O. So much so, Jordan had to support her in the elevator and down the hall.

When she opened the door, Mark rushed forward and took over, encircling Rose in his arms. He turned her toward the guest room. "Let's get you to bed."

"Hang on, Mark. I need to ask her a few questions."

Mark opened his mouth to object, but Mama Rose stayed him with her hand on his arm. "What can I do, Jordan?"

"Tell me everything you remember, from the time they pulled you into the car until the minute they let you out at the rendezvous."

Mama Rose sat on the sofa, and Jordan watched with admiration while Rose pulled herself together and began to talk. She told of a frightening, bumpy ride, of being blindfolded and gagged in the backseat of the Expedition, but Rose was a sharp cookie, a writer and gatherer of details and had retained more than Jordan could have hoped for.

"There was one of those cargo-type doors. Overhead, you know. It made a clanking noise when it went up and down. I couldn't see, but I got the impression it was a big, empty place. And it smelled funny. I know you're going to think I've gone crackers, but it smelled like coffee. Coffee. I swear. And I heard trains nearby."

THERE WAS MORE, BUT Jordan latched onto the part about the big, empty place near the railroad tracks that smelled like coffee. A warehouse. They'd taken Rose to a warehouse, and chances were good that Eddie was in the same place.

Jordan glanced at the clock. Three twenty, still the middle of the night, but she couldn't even think about being tired.

Gina came from the kitchen, a steaming cup in her hand. She set it on the dining room table. "I made coffee. Here."

Jordan drank it down—hot, strong, and black. She was lost, walking a high wire with no safety net. Eddie was gone, taken God knows where, or why—God and Tony LaSalle.

Gotta get him back. Can't let them have him. Not Eddie. Her vision blurred, eyes burning. She looked away from Gina. No tears.

"Where's my grandma?" Gina asked.

Jordan tilted her head toward the spare bedroom. "Mark's trying to get her calmed down."

"The creep didn't hurt her, did he?"

Jordan shook her head.

"How is she?" Gina asked.

"A wreck." *Aren't we all?*

Gina hesitated before she asked, "Uncle Eddie?"

Jordan couldn't bring herself to answer, but apparently she didn't have to. Gina looked into her eyes and burst into tears.

A knock came at the door. Jordan beat Gina to it.

Coop stood at the threshold, looking sleepy, ruffled, and cherubic. A red and black motorcycle helmet was tucked under his arm.

His blue eyes were full of sympathy and concern. He stepped inside, and Gina fell into his arms, sobbing.

Really? So soon? They'd only known each other three days. Were they seriously an item already? Eddie wouldn't like it. She swallowed hard and sent a silent prayer he'd have the chance to grouse about his precious niece and the cute ex-con.

Over Gina's head, Coop's eyes asked the question.

Jordan crossed the room and sat in Eddie's horrible orange chair. She'd always hated it, but would have to admit to Eddie that while it was ugly as hell, it was comfortable as an old shoe. Again, a silent plea, *Dear God, please let me have the chance to tell him.*

She looked up at Coop. "Tank and Diego called about twenty minutes ago. They found his clothes, the tracker still in his jeans pocket, piled in the parking lot at Papago Park. They took him, Coop. We don't know where."

Gina sniffed and pulled away from Coop. "Tell us what to do."

That was the question, wasn't it? What should they do? What should any of them do? "Stay here with Mama Rose. She doesn't leave here, you understand?"

The two nodded.

"Eddie's computer is in his den. You two see what you can find out about LaSalle. I want to know everything you find, everything. You never know what might turn out to be a lead." She reached in her jeans for Eddie's keys. "Check the files on the outside chance he's stockpiled information on LaSalle."

Gina took Coop by the hand and started off down the hall toward the den. She turned back. "Where are you going?"

"Downtown, to see the only person with enough guts to get me what I need: Sofia Vercelli."

Chapter 26

IT WAS COLD AND dark and smelled like a dustbin and something else. Coffee. Coffee?

When he didn't hear anything, Eddie waited then opened his eyes.

Flat on his back in his boxers. A stainless steel hospital surgical table. Cold as hell.

An IV drip was hooked up to his right arm, chilling him from the inside out. He couldn't move, except with an intense effort of concentration. Even then his motions were tiny, nearly imperceptible. *What the …? Drugged. They drugged me.*

He shifted his eyes to inspect his surroundings. His first impression was of a big, hollow space. Empty gorilla shelves here and there told him he was in a warehouse or storage space. At second story height, several big rectangular windows revealed night sky barely visible through the dirt and grime. He could make out letters painted on the glass: Cumberland Distributors. From the looks of it, this might be one of the vacant warehouses where Tony LaSalle brought his victims to convince them to do what he and Anthony Vercelli wanted them to do. From their history together, Eddie knew LaSalle liked privacy when he worked.

Off to one side, a man sat by a small table. A camping lantern cast white light across the surface of the table and onto the man's torso. He held an open comic book in front of him. *Thor*.

Guarded. Right. Trouble with being kidnapped by someone you'd worked with in the past was that the kidnapper knew your moves. No way Tony would leave him alone. This guy wore green scrubs. LaSalle had provided him with his own friggin' nurse.

His face hurt—stiff and probably bruised. The asshole hit him when he couldn't hit back. *Coward.* He tasted blood.

Feet bound—duct tape maybe. Arms strapped down. Some kind of wide band crossed his midsection, lashing him to the table. It was obvious LaSalle was scared of him. Eddie would have laughed if he could. It was complete overkill. He couldn't even move his little finger.

The comic book fell to the floor. The man stood and crossed to stand over Eddie. His male nurse was a big Latino—a big smiling Latino. "*Buenos dias,* dude. Rise and shine. Time to wake up and smell the burritos." He reached into his pocket, took out his cell and dialed. "He's up, boss. Got it. See you then."

He moved closer and elbowed Eddie in the ribs, hard. It hurt like hell.

"Boss is on his way. He's got big plans for you."

A shiver ran through him. Tony LaSalle knew a thousand and one ways to cause pain. He wasn't looking forward to the coming ordeal. Too bad they hadn't drugged him with something to kill the pain.

But one of the things that scared him most was, he didn't have the first clue what LaSalle wanted or needed from him. Revenge. Sure. He knew LaSalle blamed him for the time he had to spend in prison. But why not just shoot his ass and be done with it? Why this elaborate scheme? And why now?

SOFIA VERCELLI LIVED IN a high-rise condo near downtown Scottsdale in the Camelback corridor, eight stories up, overlooking the canal.

Even Jordan was impressed. The place must have set Daddy back a few million.

Jordan steeled herself, hating what she was about to do but rang the doorbell anyway. *Stop whining and cowgirl up.*

Sofia opened the door and her eyes grew wide. "Wow. You look like hell. Here for grooming tips?"

Jordan bristled, but held in a retort. She had to admit Sofia did look really good for seven in the morning. Her hair was pulled back in a high ponytail. Her skin was clean and healthy-looking. She wore tight-fitting spin pants and a Lycra tank. She held a half-empty bottle of Fiji water in one hand. She looked gorgeous, no surprise, and normal, big surprise. No trace of the bimbo Jordan met in Eddie's apartment. Was that only a few days ago? It seemed like a lifetime.

"Eddie's in trouble."

Without a word, Sofia stepped back and pulled the door open wide.

Jordan walked in. The door shut behind her.

Sofia turned to her. "Tell me."

Sofia seemed to hang on Jordan's every word.

When she finished, Sofia said, "Wait here," and left the room.

In less than a minute she came back shrugging into a Lucky Brand cropped hoodie, her purse and car keys in one hand.

"Let's go."

"Where?"

"Where do you think? To my dad's."

THE BIG LATINO FROM the parking lot was hammering at him like a union carpenter. His fist sailed into Eddie's face again. His head jerked back with the force.

His face felt huge; the skin was tight. His eyes were so swollen, he could hardly see, and his vision pulsed with the rhythm of the throbbing in his head. His nose was so battered, he could hardly breathe through it, and air came to him in wet, shallow gulps through his mouth.

Earlier they'd moved him from the bed to a chair. Like the big bad wolf, *all the better to beat the bejeezus out of you, my dear.*

Tony stood a few feet away, but the ringing in Eddie's ears made him sound like he was in a tunnel. "Good enough for now, Angel."

Angel? Ironic. Eddie smiled. At least he thought he managed it; it hurt.

"How you feeling, asshole?" Tony walked around him.

Eddie's gaze could only track him part of the way.

The toe of Tony's boot smashed into Eddie's shin.

Eddie groaned. Fun and games courtesy of Tony "The Prick" LaSalle.

"Look at you now, hot stuff," Tony went on, "The old man always thought you were his golden boy, his special apprentice, his protégé. Only you weren't, were you? He found out you're nothing but a coward."

Says the hero who shoots 'em in the back.

LaSalle went on. "You didn't have the stomach … or the balls to get the job done. You ran. *Coward.*"

The boot landed on Eddie's leg again. He swallowed the pain. His throat was so dry it was as if he had a mouthful of dirt. "Owe you for Muggs, Tony. I'll come for you."

"I'll take my chances, but I'm not gonna kill you. You're too valuable to me. You tell me where my gold coins are, and you boogie out of here just like Kevin Bacon."

Did I hear him right? "Gold coins?"

LaSalle leaned in until Eddie could smell the garlic on his breath. "What did you do with them?"

"I ain't got 'em." He could barely hear his own voice. "Been looking for them myself."

"Don't bother lying. I saw you. At Frankie's place," Tony hissed, and his spittle made Eddie turn his head. "I saw you leave. You had one of those little cases in one hand and the bag with the rest of them in the other."

Eddie managed to shake his head a little. *The drugs must be wearing off.*

LaSalle smacked him on top of the head. It hurt, but Eddie went on, "I don't have them, and I don't know where they are."

Tony's voice was tight and low. "You better be giving it to me straight. If Frankie don't still have them, I'm coming back here. I'll beat the truth out of you, and you won't like my methods."

It struck him then. Frankie. Diego better be on his toes. Trouble was heading for Frankie and for Diego, too, if he was on the job like he was supposed to be.

Eddie shivered, but this time it wasn't from the cold.

Chapter 27

⌐

BY THE TIME SOFIA drove Jordan to the country club in her 550 SL on Friday morning, Anthony was already at the nineteenth hole with a Mimosa and a couple of *croissants* in front of him.

He looked up in surprise as the two women approached. And why not? His daughter and Jordan Welsh were probably the last two people on earth he ever expected to see together.

Sofia wasted no time in telling her father what she knew. Jordan kept quiet, allowing the apple of her daddy's eye to plead her case.

Vercelli's face hardened as his daughter's tale progressed. When she finished, he set his jaw. "Tony hasn't shown up for work for a couple of days. Haven't seen or heard from him since Wednesday morning. And after what you told us about him and the cartel, we been looking." His gaze swept over the expansive greens, but he didn't appear to be seeing them. He reached for his cellphone. "I'm declaring war against Tony LaSalle. He crossed the line with the cartel, but he's really screwed up now. Eddie's like family to me. You don't mess with family and live."

*　*　*

SOFIA DROVE TWENTY MILES an hour over the speed limit. Was it an indication of how worried she was about Eddie, or was it just the way she always drove?

Jordan dialed Gina, who answered right away with, "Did you find him?"

Her heart sank. "No. I was calling to see if you had anything. I'm doing everything I know to do, but I'm way open to suggestions."

"Coop's in the process of hacking LaSalle's email and social media. We thought maybe we'd get lucky with a name or a face there."

Jordan shook her head. Reduced to trolling Facebook. *What next?*

"Tank and Diego are hitting up every old contact of Eddie's. They thought maybe Tony told somebody in Vercelli's organization what he planned."

"If so, we'd know already. Vercelli's got everybody in town looking for LaSalle."

Gina continued, "I called every investigator on my contacts list. They're looking and checking for anything and everything related to Tony LaSalle."

Jordan sighed. "How's Mama Rose?"

"She's sleeping. Mark got her quiet and convinced her to take a pill. She's not handling it well, Jordan, not handling it at all."

"I figured as much."

"My mom's on her way here." Gina didn't sound like this was a good thing. "I tried to stop her, but it was too late. She doesn't know anything about all the trouble. She's just coming for the wedding."

"It is what it is," Jordan said. "Maybe she'll comfort Mama Rose."

Jordan couldn't think of anything else to say, but didn't want to hang up. Gina was a connection to Eddie, a close connection, and something about talking to her was comforting. "Let me know if anybody finds out anything. Someone somewhere has a list of who this guy hangs with, does business with. If we can get it, we can find Eddie."

She disconnected. It all came crashing down onto her at once. She had gone to Anthony Vercelli, a man with little conscience and a high tolerance for violence. Anthony Vercelli, without whom Eddie wouldn't even be in this mess. She'd had to ask him for his help. And now she was in a car with Sofia, Eddie's old girlfriend. They had to find him and fast, before Tony killed him. She'd avoided thinking about it until just that moment.

Tony intended to kill Eddie. Why else would he have taken him?

What other explanation was there? Did he want money? He hadn't asked for it. Did he want revenge? Then why not just kill him on the spot?

A sob tore from her. *Eddie.* She could lose Eddie, who loved her and had her back, who made her laugh, and supported her every dream.

As much as she hated crying in front of Sofia, once the first sob broke loose, another followed. Before she knew it, she was crying and moaning, sobbing like a child.

Sofia accelerated to eighty-five and passed three cars as she took the exit for Chaparral then drove straight to her condominium.

Jordan reached for her keys, but Sofia laid her hand on top of hers. "Look, Jordan, you're in no shape to drive. Come upstairs until you—"

Jordan snapped, "Until I what? Until I settle down?" She was instantly sorry. Sofia was right. She was a mess.

Without another word, she fell in step beside Sofia, and the two women took the elevator up to Sofia's condo.

Two fingers of Hennessy XO in a brandy snifter went down between hiccups. It did calm her. When Sofia offered a second pour, Jordan didn't object.

She sat back on the grass-green sofa and tucked an accent

pillow against her chest. "Thanks for the drink. It helped."

She looked at the woman swirling the amber liquid in her own glass.

"Sofia?"

She turned and Jordan was struck yet again by how much prettier she was without all the glitter, glamour, and bling.

Jordan chose each word carefully. This could turn out to be some thin ice if word got back to Vercelli she was digging into his business. "What sent LaSalle to prison? What was the thing Eddie refused to do for your father?"

Sofia looked into the glass and kept swirling. "It was a vendetta. Not just any vendetta. It was important to Poppy." She sat down on a stool by the granite bar counter. "Did you know about my brother?"

Jordan shook her head. "Eddie doesn't like to talk about his previous life." She consciously avoided the word *didn't*.

"He was killed. Murdered. That's how I came to know anything at all about the family business. I was always kept away, at arm's length—the classic little mafia princess. But after Michael died, I thought maybe Poppy would want me to be next in line to take over. He doesn't know I looked into things, still thinks I'm his innocent little girl. But I know a lot more than he thinks I do."

Jordan listened and considered Sofia's words. "You plan on taking over your father's business some day?"

"No," Sofia said. "After what I learned, I want to stay as far away from those people as possible. My father included."

They sat in silence for a few moments, Jordan digesting this interesting bit of insight into Sofia's personality. Sofia was lost in her own thoughts.

"Michael was five years older than I am." Sofia's voice was quiet. "You should have seen my brother. He was beautiful for a man, like an angel." She had a faraway look in her eyes. "He worked for the family business, but his heart wasn't in it. He never was much good at it and the poor guy was just in the wrong place at the wrong time. He got involved in a business deal with one of Poppy's enemies. Poppy put a stop to it. He couldn't take Michael back into the business after that. Couldn't trust him. The other side, they didn't want him either. They killed him to get back at my father. The code demands an eye for an eye. The man who murdered my brother, his son was only seventeen years old. He was part of the criminal activities, but still just a kid."

Jordan caught her breath.

Sofia looked at her and nodded. "You heard right. My father asked Eddie, his enforcer, to make a hit on a teenager. No way Eddie would do it. He refused."

Jordan filled in the blanks. "But LaSalle didn't."

"Tony went to jail."

"And he blamed it on Eddie, so he wants payback and he's taking it out of Eddie's hide."

Sofia whistled through her teeth. "Big mistake. Tony ought to know better. Any loyalty Poppy might have for him flew out the window when he went after Eddie. Poppy loves Eddie. All hell's about to rain down on Tony LaSalle."

"Good," Jordan said. "Couldn't happen to a nicer guy."

SHE LEFT SOFIA'S AND drove around town for more than two hours, aimlessly, not sure where she was going or why. She only knew she had to do something.

Eventually, drained and exhausted, Jordan went to the office and checked in with everyone, one by one. Gina and Coop, Tank and Diego. Nobody had made any progress at all.

Inside of a half hour, Tank showed up.

"Eddie would want y'all covered. If nobody else is available, I'm hanging around."

She looked up at Tank, who sat down across the room, fiddling with his keys. "You look like something the cat dragged home," he said.

"Sweet talk, Tank?"

"No, I'm serious. Y'all need to go home."

"I want to be here if Eddie … if we hear anything."

Her phone rang, *Bad Boys*. Detective Murphy. Ann. As far as Jordan knew, Ann hadn't been told of Eddie's abduction. All the same, she fell on the phone like a chocolate addict on a BOGO day at a Godiva store.

Jordan took a couple of deep breaths and centered herself. "Ann. What's up?"

"Just calling to check in. We can't find a trace of this LaSalle character. You get anything?

"Nothing. It's like he's gone into witness protection or something."

"Funny," Ann said. "Hilarious. Call me if you get anything."

"You too."

She looked up to see Tank staring at her speculatively. "She doesn't know about Eddie, does she?" he said. "You haven't told her."

Jordan shook her head. "No."

"Why not?"

"Cops, Tank. I know Annie. She'd get right into the middle of things. She's a cop down to her handcuff keys. She pulls up someplace with a squad of cruisers, lights flashing, sirens blaring, you know what happens to Eddie?"

Tank nodded.

"I can't tell her. She could get him killed trying to help." Her nose stung and her eyes burned. She raised a trembling hand to wipe away any tears that might spill over in front of her friend and employee.

Tank got up and crossed the room. He took hold of her by the elbow and pulled her up, picked up her phone and handbag off the desk and led her to the front door.

"Go home, Miss Jordan. Please. Get some rest."

Chapter 28

IT WAS SEVEN FRIDAY night and Jordan had just drained her second glass of wine. She sat at the kitchen table. The only light in the room came from the refrigerator panel and backyard ground lights, which cast a dim glow through the window over the sink. The dirty dishes stacked there reminded her that Hannah, her housekeeper, would be back at work on Monday after a two week visit to her sister in San Diego. Maybe Jordan would load the dishwasher later. Maybe. It wasn't high on her priority list just now.

The sight of the house, so quiet and dark, comforted her tired soul. But Eddie was out there somewhere, and she needed to leave the peace she found here to save him.

She was contemplating a third glass of wine when the doorbell rang.

She almost didn't answer, then reconsidered on the outside chance it could be about Eddie.

Her face must have fallen dramatically when she opened the door because her mother said, "Really? With that face, I'm guessing I'm not who you were expecting." She pushed into the house, carrying several Neiman Marcus garment bags over her shoulder.

"I knew you would be too busy to go try on dresses for the wedding, so I brought the dresses to you. Wait until you get a look at them. Stunning. You'll knock Eddie's eyes out when he sees you." She looked around. "He isn't here, is he?"

Jordan burst into racking sobs. Her nose ran, tears streamed down her cheeks, and her throat closed up.

Mary dropped the bags where she stood and pulled her daughter into her arms. "Oh my God, honey. What's wrong?"

"Eddie, Mom. He's missing. He's …."

Mary gasped and led Jordan to the sofa. "Sit." It was a command.

Mary sat beside her. "Tell me. All of it. Every single thing."

Jordan did.

When she was done and the crying had stopped, Mary reached into her handbag, took two pills from a bottle and handed them to Jordan. "You need to sleep. You're not going to be of use to anyone in the shape you're in, especially Eddie. Go to bed. Get some sleep. Go at 'em again in the morning."

Jordan was suddenly so drained she couldn't think, couldn't move, could barely keep her eyes open.

Mary helped her out of her clothes and into bed, kissed her on the forehead, and turned out the light. "I'm going to Eddie's place. Rose will need someone there who understands what she's going through. Another mother."

As Mary turned, Jordan caught her hand and brought it to her lips. "I love you, Mom."

"And I you, sweet girl." Mary bent, raised their joined hands up and kissed the back of Jordan's hand.

Sweet girl. Her mother hadn't used the pet name since she was in grade school. Sometimes the woman surprised her.

SHE CAME UP OUT of a sleep so deep it was like crawling out of a hole. What woke her? Sadie, panting. Her hot breath fanned Jordan's face.

Her head felt like she was underwater. What day was it? What time?

"What is it, girl? What's …."

She heard it this time. The doorbell. Someone leaning on it so the Westminster chimes sounded over and over again on top of each other. What? Her bedside clock showed five forty. Saturday morning. Eddie had been gone only a little over twenty-four hours. Good Lord, it seemed like weeks. Months. Could only six months have passed since she'd debated whether or not to give in to her desire for him? A sob caught in her throat. Now she couldn't begin to imagine life without him.

Moving as fast as her heavy limbs would carry her, she stumbled to the front door and didn't even take the precaution of looking through the peephole. She threw it open.

Coop, looking disheveled and tired but completely adorable in a striped tee, jean jacket, and tight Levi's, smiled with relief. "Finally. Dude, were you hibernating, or what? I was getting worried. Been laying on the doorbell maybe ten minutes or so." His eyes swept over her and bugged out. "Wow. Do you always answer the door dressed like that, Miss Welsh?" He stopped. "Oh, I guess I really caught you by surprise this early. Sorry but I got something, and you know—tick, tock." He stared pointedly at the doormat.

She was in a general state of confusion. She hadn't even bothered to throw on a robe over her T-shirt and panties.

Coop. What's he doing here? She grabbed him by the arm and pulled him in.

"Coffee," she said. "We need coffee."

He smiled and shrugged. "Cool. I could use a latte."

Fifteen minutes later she was dressed and awake. Her head hurt from the sedatives her mother had given her, but at least she'd finally been able to sleep. For once she was grateful her mother's handbag was as well stocked as the local pharmacy. This time Mary's mild hypochondria had come in handy.

Jordan never doubted her mother's love, but the evidence of

it came so rarely, she was always stunned to see it.

"So," Coop dipped his biscotti into his coffee, "this guy I knew on the inside called me up last night. He owed me one large, and when he heard we were asking around about Tony LaSalle, he saw his shot to even the score. I know it's pretty early, but I figured you'd want to hear about it."

He dipped again, and it was all Jordan could do not to snatch the cookie from his hand, grab his shirt, and force him to talk faster. "Yes, Coop. And what did he tell you?"

"He heard of this drug dealer named Reilly—Danny Reilly. He heard LaSalle's name mentioned in the same sentence with Reilly's." He scratched his head. "You know what I mean?"

"Not exactly. It would be better if you spelled it out. I'm a little slow this morning."

He nodded. "I know what you mean. I'm no good at all until I've had a shower and a latte, and have been up and cruising around for an hour or so."

"Focus, Coop. What did your friend tell you about Tony LaSalle and Danny Reilly?"

"They've been doing some business on the side for a while now. He said word on the street is Tony LaSalle and Danny Reilly have gone entrepreneurial."

She shook her head and had to admit, "I have absolutely no idea what you're talking about."

He looked straight at her, and she saw the façade he wore so easily slip away. His eyes shone clear and blue, and that high IQ spoke through them. "LaSalle's been robbing other drug dealers to supplement Reilly's goods— you know, on the side. I'm pretty sure LaSalle's boss Anthony Vercelli doesn't know about it."

"I don't suppose your friend on the inside has any idea where one might find Mr. Reilly?"

Coop nodded. "Maybe, but, Miss Welsh, this Reilly guy. Not somebody you want to fool with. He's got a rep."

"For what?"

"For being a serious guy. Serious enough to think twice before you mess with his business. Some people who did, they disappeared."

She looked at him.

He shrugged. "Just sayin'."

Jordan stood. "Drink your latte, Coop."

"Yes, ma'am," he said.

"You're coming with me."

He got up from the table, taking the time to stash a couple of extra biscotti in his jacket pocket. "Where are we going?"

She smiled. It was the first time in over two days she'd felt like it, but now she had something to smile about. A lead. They had a lead. Not much of one, but it was more than they had yesterday.

"Hunting, Coop. We're going hunting."

She tossed him the keys to her car.

WHILE COOP DROVE, JORDAN worked the phone, sending anyone with wheels out on the street to determine the whereabouts of one Danny Reilly, drug dealer.

Tank and Diego were the most likely to find him, but she also called Sofia, who promised to see to it her "Poppy" got wind of what was going on between Reilly and LaSalle.

Jordan took a few minutes to call Gina and check up on Rose.

Gina sounded a bit overwhelmed. "My mom's flight got in last night, and at six o'clock this morning your mother showed up. All three of them are in the kitchen cooking breakfast. Geez, Jordan, I think they're getting ready to feed the troops or something. Grandma wanted to cancel her wedding, but your mother convinced her you'd find Eddie alive and well in plenty of time for him to walk down the aisle with her."

COOP'S INFORMANT SAID DANNY Reilly was known to get in an hour and a half workout every morning at Blackie's Gym on the west side of town.

Jordan gave her Pilot up to Coop, whose job for the day was watching LaSalle's house. It wasn't likely Tony would be stupid enough to head back to it, but on the outside chance—

"I'm on it, boss lady." He saluted and turned like a toy soldier. It nearly broke Jordan's heart. "Boss lady" was what Eddie called her.

She rode across town with Tank.

The gym was full at seven thirty. It was one of those hardcore places. Concrete floors. The smell of sweat and stale jock straps. The grunts and clanks of uncompromising lifters. Not a female in sight, at first glance. A closer look revealed that some of the athletes in tank tops weren't macho dudes at all, but macho chicks.

"Looking for Danny Reilly," Tank said.

The counter person, a seventy-something bald guy with pecs like dinner plates, sent them to the back, where they found the man of the hour working a speed bag like a WBA champion.

He was not tall, but not really short. Maybe five ten, like her. Lean, fit.

"Danny Reilly?"

He stopped the rat-a-tat on the bag and turned. His eyes swept Jordan top to bottom.

"What can I do for you, girl?" He spoke quickly, like he had something important to say and was in a hurry to get it out. The timbre of his voice was rich and low. He wore his dark hair longish. It was wet with perspiration and curled boyishly around his face.

No doubt about it. Danny Reilly was good-looking with an irreverent twinkle in his brown eyes that promised a good time if she was up for it. She wasn't. Jordan reminded herself whom she was dealing with—the packaging might be pretty, but the contents were rancid.

She identified herself and showed him her PI license, a gesture she reserved for scumbags and known criminals. "We're looking for Tony LaSalle. It's been tossed around you might know where we can find him."

"LaSalle, you say?" His gaze shifted as he seemed to consider the name.

He turned away from the speed bag, slipped off the gloves, and began to walk casually toward the men's locker room.

He stopped at the open doorway and turned back to her, shaking his head.

She wasn't going to make it that easy for him.

She followed him inside and watched while he put a lock on one of the lockers, trying to make the action seem casual. To Jordan it seemed anything but casual.

He smiled when he saw she'd followed him in. "Okay. Yeah. I heard of Tony LaSalle, maybe even met him a time or two, but I don't know where you'd find him these days." His voice was musical and good humored, but she wasn't taken in by his charisma.

"Look, Mr. Reilly—" she began.

"My friends call me Danny Boy," he said. "Like the song?"

"Mr. Reilly, we need Tony LaSalle for something that has absolutely nothing to do with you."

He didn't blink or look away. The smile, which might be considered sweet on any other man, never wavered. "Sorry, luv. Like I said, I hear he's busy taking care of some old business—something he's wanted to take care of for a long time." Something in his eyes changed, issuing a dark challenge.

She knew he was talking about Eddie, and she knew they were done. He wouldn't give up LaSalle, but it had been worth a try.

"But …." he said.

Her heart thumped. Maybe she'd read him wrong.

"… everything is negotiable. If the offer's good enough, I might be willing to see if I could locate LaSalle."

She shook her head. "I'm not all that good at negotiation unless I'm sure what's being offered is worth it."

"A shame. I bet we could make it worthwhile for both of us."

Tank bristled, looking as if he wanted to apply a little muscle to the conversation. She laid her hand on his arm and shook her head. "Thanks anyway, Mr. Reilly." As she turned to go she handed him her card. "Just in case."

He stuck it in the pocket of his gym shorts. As she turned away, he caught hold of her hand and wrote a phone number on the inside of her wrist. "In case you change your mind— you know, about negotiating."

Chapter 29

~

ON THEIR WAY BACK across town, a little before nine thirty Saturday morning, Jordan's phone rang.

"Jordan, it's Coop. LaSalle's here. He showed up about five minutes ago."

"Are you sure?"

"Pretty sure. Mean-looking dude in a silver Lexus."

"That would be him." She signaled Tank, who hung a right and headed south into Arcadia. "Keep your eyes open, but don't go in there. Don't approach him."

He hung up. She wasn't sure he got that last part. But Coop was a smart kid, and he knew LaSalle's real name started with a capital T for trouble.

It took less than ten minutes to get to LaSalle's place. They passed Jordan's car parked about a half block down the road. Coop wasn't in it. Not a good sign.

The garage door stood open, the garage empty. Also not a good sign.

Tank drew his piece, and he and Jordon went inside. They found Coop unconscious by the kitchen door. The picture frame with Tony's sister and niece lay beside him, the glass shattered. A bloody spot in his golden hair matched a splotch on the glass. Jordan knelt beside him.

Coop was already starting to come around. He gazed up at her, eyes unfocused, looking more like a choirboy than ever.

"Hey," she said.

"Hey."

He lifted himself onto his elbows. One look at the empty garage, and he said, "Dammit, he's gone."

She offered her hand, "Yep," and helped him to his feet. "Gone. What I want to know is what part of don't approach him you didn't understand."

He shrugged. "The door opened. He had a duffel bag like he was taking a trip. I figured he was outta here, and if I didn't do something, we'd never get Eddie back."

"But you should have followed him, kid, not rode in on your white charger and tried to take him down. Some serious training is in your future."

If LaSalle was packed and leaving, there was a good chance Coop was right. It made her sick to her stomach, but Eddie could already be dead. No. She couldn't go there. She had to believe Eddie was locked up somewhere, unable to get out but still alive.

Tank came out. She looked up. He shook his head. "He's gone. He's not coming back here." Their eyes met. He thought Eddie might already be dead, too. But she could see that like her, he pushed the thought away. "We'll get him back, Miss Jordan. Don't worry. Eddie's a survivor. LaSalle ain't half the man he is. He can't beat him."

EDDIE HURT ALL OVER. The IV was gone. His wrists were taped to the arms of the chair with duct tape. He could hardly hold his head up, but the drug was definitely wearing off, and he could feel his limbs again. If he wasn't taped down, he was sure he'd be able to move.

The next time one of them came at him, they'd have a harder time. No doubt about it.

But he had no delusions. One of these times, Tony would kill him. Tony wanted the coins he stole, and the only thing keeping Eddie alive was that LaSalle believed he knew where they were. If he couldn't figure a way out of this mess or if no one found him in time, he'd die in this place. And at the moment he was fresh out of ideas.

One of the front overhead doors clanked then jerked up slowly. Eddie looked up, recognizing LaSalle's silhouette against the afternoon sun, and the swagger in his gait as he crossed the big empty space.

"Eddie, my man." He laughed. "You're in a lot of trouble. Your girlfriend didn't have them, which must mean—"

No. A voice screamed inside Eddie's head. He hadn't gotten to … "Jordan? You were with—?"

"Jordan? Hell, no," LaSalle said. "Should I have been? Does she know where they are? Frankie sure as hell doesn't have 'em. She would have given them up if she did. Which means you're on, Marino."

Eddie wished he could get his hands around Tony's throat. If the piece of shit got to Frankie, he might have hurt Diego, or worse. And now even Jordan was on his radar. Look what his love for Jordan had brought her. Her very life was in danger. "You're going to have to kill me, Tony. Because if you don't, I'm going to kill you." His voice was hoarse, and it hurt just to talk.

Tony snorted. "No problem. I'm accommodating." He reached into his pocket, took out a pair of leather driving gloves and slipped them on. He flexed his fingers, grinned, and curled his right hand into a fist.

The watch-without-hands tattoo caught Eddie's eye. Tony must have noticed him staring at it. "You like? Just a little keepsake of the hard time I did because you punked out."

Eddie kept quiet. If he mentioned his familiarity with it, he'd be painting a target on Coop's back.

"Every time I look at it," Tony went on, "I think of you, Marino."

A blow to his gut caught Eddie unprepared the first time, but he clenched, and the second and subsequent blows weren't as damaging.

Nothing he could do about the sideways blows to his kidneys, nothing except try not to pass out. Tony was enjoying himself. The bastard took pleasure in each excruciating hit to his torso.

When Tony finished he was breathing harder than Eddie. For the first time Eddie was grateful he was strapped to the chair. If not, he was pretty sure he'd have fallen out of it.

"How was it?" Tony asked. "Up to your standards?"

Eddie glared up at him wordlessly.

Tony went on, "I have to say you're tougher than your pussy friend who took my blade for you at the museum. Not too smart a guy. Walked right up to him, said, 'Hey ya, Muggs. How's it hanging?' The look on his face was priceless when I stuck him. Poor bastard never even had a chance to react."

Eddie's stomach roiled, and rage boiled up in him like lava.

"Yeah. He whimpered like a baby before he finally gave it up. Too bad he wasn't stoic and brave like you." LaSalle's laughter burned in Eddie's gut like a lit fuse.

"Or brave like you?" Eddie asked. "I heard you shot both Wasserstein and his kid in the back."

Tony snarled and backhanded Eddie across the face. The leather stung like a firebrand.

"I know what you're trying to do, Marino. You can say anything you want to me, but I told you, I'm not going to kill you until I get what I want. I gotta get those coins back. I owe a lot of money to all the wrong people, and if I can't write 'em a check, they're going to bury my ass."

He looked at Eddie long and hard. "You know, if I don't scare you, maybe that long, tall drink of water you're shacked up with will feel differently. Maybe you told her what you did with the coins."

Eddie's heart lurched and went into double-time. "Bet you

won't be such a big man when Vercelli catches up to you," he said.

Something flickered in Tony's eyes—if not fear, at least anxiety. Good. Eddie tried a laugh.

Tony glanced at his watch. "Vercelli won't get a shot at me. Believe it or not, he's not the worst of my worries. If I don't pay back the drug cartels for the goods I stole from them, I'm screwed. My time's almost up with them, and if I can't get to the coins, I gotta leave town." He tapped the tattoo on his wrist. "Be thinking if you want to save your woman. Tick-tock, Eddie. Tick-tock."

LaSalle turned and walked out of the warehouse. The overhead door closed behind him and shut with a clank.

Was he going after Jordan? It didn't sound like the smart move, and Tony had never been stupid—or maybe he was. Stealing from Vercelli *and* the Mexican drug cartels? Not exactly Mensa material. He was worried about Jordan, but hadn't sensed much conviction behind Tony's threat to go after her. Still, just the thought made Eddie sick to his stomach.

AFTER A STOP AT Urgent Care, where Coop was bandaged and given a clean bill of health, Jordan drove him back to her place, where he picked up his bike and left for Eddie's to spell Gina.

It was around five Saturday afternoon before she had a chance to sit and scarf down a PB&J sandwich while Sadie devoured a bowl of kibble. Sadie finished and came for love, laying her head on Jordan's knee. Big, mournful eyes stared up at her with way more understanding than Jordan would have thought possible.

"I'm gonna get him back, girl. Don't you worry."

A hot shower revitalized her, and she stepped from the steam, ready to hit it again.

There was a voicemail from Diego. "Jordan, get down to All Saints Hospital on Dunlap ASAP. I'm here with Frankie

Manheim. LaSalle broke into her place. *El cobarde* beat her pretty bad."

Jordan threw on a pair of clean jeans, a long-sleeved T-shirt, and Doc Martens and ran out the door.

Chapter 30

～

DIEGO MET HER OUTSIDE the ER entrance of the hospital. "Is she hurt bad?" Jordan asked.

He nodded. "Worked her over pretty good. They're admitting her for overnight observation."

"What did they want?"

Diego took her by the hand. "Come with me. She can tell you."

FRANKIE'S FACE WAS BLACK and blue, green and purple, her eyes puffy. Cuts over her left brow and upper lip were closed with butterfly bandages. Her left arm was in a sling.

Her eyes were closed when they walked in.

"Is she unconscious?" Jordan whispered.

He shook his head. "Frankie?"

Her eyes opened.

Jordan went to one side of the bed, Diego the other.

"What happened, Frankie?" Jordan asked.

Frankie's eyes shifted to Diego.

When he nodded at Frankie, she turned back to Jordan and began, "The alarm went off at the store. We've had some trouble with it lately, so when the PD called, I told them not to bother and I went down to check it out. Tony LaSalle was waiting for me. He hadn't found what he was looking for so he made me drive back to my house with him. I wouldn't tell him where to look. He took his fist to me. When that didn't do the trick either, he stood on my shoulder and pulled on my arm." She glanced at the sling supporting her arm. "Shoulder popped out. I couldn't take it. I was out like a light for a while. When I woke up, the house looked like a tornado had blown through. God, what a mess. I called Diego. Sweet boy. He came right away and brought me here."

Jordan gave her a serious look. "You're lucky to make it out alive, Frankie. I hear not everyone who comes up against Tony LaSalle does." She waited a moment. "What was he looking for? The Dahlonega coins he gave you?"

Frankie snorted then grimaced. "Ow." She took a couple of deep breaths. "Not just those two I showed you, missy, the whole kit and caboodle. I had the whole collection. He left 'em with me to sell. I hid 'em. And why not? Why shouldn't I have a piece of the pie, especially, if I'm the one who's taking the risks?" She smiled. "I was close to unloading them, too. Sap in Texas was willing to pay fifty cents on the dollar. LaSalle wanted twenty-five. I stood to make a fortune."

Jordan was stuck back on "hid them." The complete set? Frankie had the entire Golden Dream collection the whole time? Sly fox. She'd been holding out on everybody. It nearly got her killed, too.

"Where'd you stash them?" Jordan asked.

Frankie set her jaw and thrust out her lower lip, a portrait of defiance.

It didn't look like she was in the mood to share. *At least not with me.*

Jordan looked up and caught Diego's eye. She nodded her head slightly.

He nodded back then moved closer to Frankie, lifted her

right hand, and held it between both of his.

"You need to tell us, Miz Manheim, for your own safety. Even I can't protect you now, not while you have those stolen coins in your possession."

She stared deep into his eyes as if she'd do just about anything for him. And it looked like she would. "The rear compartment of your Jeep, Diego honey, under the flappy thing in the very back."

Diego's jaw dropped.

Jordan's, too.

They looked at each other.

"You mean I've been driving around with them since ...."

Frankie nodded. "Since the first day you showed up at the store."

A HALF HOUR LATER they walked back through the ER entrance. The lights cast a yellow glow over the hospital parking lot. Jordan and Diego crossed to where he'd parked his Jeep Wrangler. Diego poked along behind Jordan, quiet, his head hanging.

"You coming or not?" Jordan turned around. "What's up with you?"

He looked up at her, his expression troubled. "I let her down."

It took a second for her to comprehend what he was talking about. "Oh, you mean Frankie. How'd you let her down?" Then she got it. "This wasn't your fault. You couldn't stay with her day and night. And if I had a choice, I'd rather she be lying in that bed, not you."

His doubtful look said he still wasn't convinced.

"Look. If she hadn't taken the coins from LaSalle to start with, she wouldn't be in this position. She made her bed, now she has to lie ...." She paused. *Oh my God. I sound just like my mother.* "Well, you know what I mean." *Besides*, she thought, *we needed you to be out looking for Eddie.*

He swung the tailgate aside and lifted the carpet flap over

the tire iron compartment. The beam of a small flashlight illuminated the dark cubicle, revealing a first aid kit, a couple of tools, and a medium-sized duffle bag. It looked like the bag Eddie carried with him sometimes. He removed the bag, set it on the trailer hitch, unzipped it, and shined the light on it.

Even though they had a good idea what they'd find, the reflection off the acrylic cases and gold coins took them by surprise.

Diego whistled.

Jordan said, "Well, would you look at that."

After a minute, Diego turned to her. "You know what this means, right?"

Jordan had no idea.

"It means I'm screwed."

She nodded. He was right. If they turned the coins in to the police, even if they gave up Frankie, Diego would be implicated. There was no way to prove he had no prior knowledge of the stolen collection being placed in his car. It was vital the coins be recovered for the sake of the company's reputation, also vital they be credited with the find.

"What are we going to do?" he asked.

Before she even had a chance to think about it, her phone rang. "Fire" by the Ohio Players. It was Steve Keegan.

"Hi, Steve. I'm kind of in the middle of something."

"I may know where Eddie is."

"You what?" He had her complete attention. "Tell me," she said.

"I'll do you one better. I'll show you."

ALMOST EIGHT O'CLOCK SATURDAY night and Jordan and Diego were sitting in Steve Keegan's dilapidated old '82 Chevy Suburban, parked in a vacant lot in the warehouse district near the railroad spur. The night air was brisk, but they had rolled down all the windows to keep from suffocating in the dusty, smelly interior. The old car was acrid with the odor of smoke and chemicals from having been present at the site of dozens, if not hundreds of fires. It had been left sitting in the brutal Arizona sun for so many years, the metallic paint was peeling off the hood. Whenever Steve drove down the street, he said he could see bits of the paint flaking off. He called it "The Flake-Mobile."

Steve was in the driver's seat. Moonlight glinted off his glasses and balding head. His round belly nearly met the steering wheel. "I got word you were looking into Danny Reilly as well as hunting for warehouses where LaSalle might have taken Eddie," Steve said. "There was this warehouse fire pretty close to here, total loss. The holding company that owned it was so badly put together I only had to go down one layer to find this Danny Reilly character. We're pretty sure the fire was set by one of the Mexican cartel's local boys. Reilly's in business against them."

"Yes," Jordan said. "We've heard that, too."

"Within a few months of the other place burning down, records showed that the same holding company had purchased another warehouse."

Jordan listened to every word, every syllable. Steve wasn't the kind of guy to come to them with information unless he was dead solid. "And where is this new place?"

He raised his hand and pointed. "Right over there."

Jordan followed his finger to a big building, fifty or seventy-five yards across the way. Square, high windows, cargo doors. Standard warehouse fare.

Something inside her began to vibrate. Eddie was there.

Like a mind reader, Steve posed the question, "What are you going to do if you're too late? What if LaSalle's already killed him?"

She glared at him, although he probably couldn't tell in the dark. "Don't say that. Don't even think it."

"Inappropriate, man," Diego said. "You're talking about

Eddie Marino. It would take more than Tony LaSalle can put together to off Eddie Marino."

"He's still alive, Steve." Jordan was surprised at the conviction in her own voice. "I'd know if he wasn't. I'd feel it." But she still prayed she was right.

She turned to the backseat where Diego sat on exposed foam rubber. "Diego?"

Without a word, he reached to the floorboard and came up with the thermal imager. She opened the car door and got out.

She'd used the long-range bi-ocular thermal imaging camera on a couple of other cases. It was a tool Eddie swore by and with any luck would again, soon. She raised it to her eyes, aimed it at the warehouse, and switched it on.

She heard Steve and Diego get out and quietly click their car doors shut.

Her vision was immediately filled with a kaleidoscope of purples, blues, yellows, reds, and greens. The warmer yellow images revealed two human beings. Both appeared to be male. One paced. It looked like he might have been talking on a cell phone. The second figure sat slouched in a chair, unmoving. She caught her breath. Eddie. It was Eddie. The heat signature indicated he was alive, but the fact that he didn't seem to be moving worried her.

"I see him," she said.

Behind her, Diego let out a breath.

She handed him the camera and waited.

"Way to go, Marino," Diego crowed.

"What?" She jerked around.

"He moved. The guy in the chair, he moved."

Eddie was alive. Something gave way inside her, and her eyes filled with tears of relief.

In the moonlight, she and Diego stared at each other, sharing a moment of silent communication.

Diego nodded.

"Let's get busy," she said.

Chapter 31

~

EDDIE'S PLACE HAD NEVER been so full.

Jordan and Diego arrived to find Tank, Coop, and Gina there as Jordan had requested. Mama Rose, Mary, Mark, and last but not least, Theresa. Oh, yes, Theresa.

Jordan hadn't met Eddie's sister before. All she knew about Theresa was she was currently single and being supported by Eddie. She'd been married three times, each husband a bigger loser than the one before him. Theresa was a licensed cosmetologist. Haircuts, color, and mani-pedis, but six months seemed to be the expiration date on any job she took.

"Oh my gawd!" Theresa rushed forward when Jordan, exhausted and stressed, came through Eddie's door with Diego.

Jordan cringed and pulled away, only to be embraced again.

"I've heard so much about you, Jordan." She burst into tears. "Oh, Eddie, Eddie!"

Gina came forward to untangle her mother from Jordan. "Mom, let's give Jordan a break."

Theresa nodded, pulled a Kleenex from her jeans pocket, and blew her nose, loudly. She leaned dramatically against Gina as the two cleared a path for Jordan to head to the back of the condo where Mama Rose and Mary sat at the dining room table.

Jordan collapsed into a chair between the two matrons. Mary looked tired and anxious. It was the first time for as long as Jordan could remember she'd seen her mother with messy hair and a naked face.

Rose, too, looked like she'd aged ten years. Jordan took hold of her hand and squeezed.

She looked first at Mary, then at Rose. "I know where he is, and I know he's alive," she said. "Eddie's alive."

Rose began to whimper then to cry. Mary got up, circled the table and embraced Rose from behind. "There, there, honey. You cry. You've been so brave and so strong for your son. Jordan's going to get him back. You can let go now."

Jordan stared at her mother. Every once in a while the heart behind the Mary Welsh who spent tireless hours at work for her charity programs surfaced. When it did, it was magnificent.

"Love you, Mom," she said softly.

Mary looked up and nodded.

Jordan's phone rang. Generic. Maybe this was the return call she'd been waiting for. She stood, opened the arcadia door behind her and went outside to answer it.

"Jordan Welsh?" The voice was bright, cheerful.

"Danny Reilly," she said. "Thanks for calling me back."

"How could I resist, Jordan? You come into my life with those long legs and those big dreamy eyes. Of course I'd call you back. I hope you're not going to try to persuade me to narc out that guy you asked about. I told you this morning I wouldn't do it." He sighed so dramatically she could just imagine him pouting. "You've broken my heart, sweetie. I thought maybe you'd been thinking about me all day like I've been thinking about you."

He was leading her to exactly where she wanted to take him. She had indeed been thinking about him all day, but probably not the way he imagined. When she saw how protective he was of his gym locker, an idea had struck her. Maybe struck wasn't a good choice of words because this one might be the idea to actually come back and knock her for a loop. It occurred to her that if this guy was all hot and bothered about her, there might be a way she could use it against him.

"I *was* thinking about you," she paused then added, "Danny."

He was quiet for a while, then, "In a good way I hope."

She tried her sexy voice, even if it always sounded dumb to her. "Oh, yes, a very good way. I thought about what you said about negotiating, making it worthwhile for everyone concerned. Maybe we could meet somewhere." Her heart raced. She had never been good at this kind of game.

But it seemed to be working.

He sounded cocky, satisfied with himself. "I like the sound of that. Name it, and I'll show up."

She smiled to herself. "There's this place I've been wanting to try …."

BACK INSIDE, A BREAD line had formed in the kitchen, where Theresa and Mary were dishing up penne pasta and shrimp sautéed in butter and garlic. A couple of bottles of red wine, two baguettes, and a stick of butter sat on the bar. It smelled divine, and it looked like a scene straight out of *The Godfather*.

Jordan joined the others. It was serious business. No one spoke as they chowed down.

Mama Rose complained she felt like road kill and wanted to go back to her hotel and shower. Jordan called in the hard case Diego hired to protect Rose and sent him with Rose, Mark, Gina, and Mary over to their hotel.

Jordan turned to Theresa. "Maybe you'd like to go with them."

"What," Theresa said, "and miss all the action?"

Jordan shrugged. Theresa didn't seem like the brightest bulb in the marquee. Maybe she wouldn't catch on to the conversation.

She spoke to the crew. "Boys, we need to be sure our alibis for tonight are solid."

"Alibi? Do I need one, too?" Theresa asked.

Jordan just sighed then went on, "We'll be conspicuous and public. That should be fine."

Tank and Diego looked at each other, then at her. "But, Miss Jordan, we are going to get Eddie back."

Confusion was written on their faces—furrowed brows, pursed lips. Tank stood and began to pace. "We have to be there. Eddie's our—"

"He's important to me too, Tank," Jordan said. "Did you forget?"

It was obvious both men were barely holding it together. She had to lay it out for them, or she'd lose the argument, and they'd be on their way to the warehouse.

Diego narrowed his eyes. "But we're going to get him. Right? Somebody has to go after Eddie."

"Somebody is going after Eddie, but it won't be us."

Chapter 32

TIME TO GET READY for her *date* with Danny Reilly. A plan was in place to rescue Eddie, but just in case, she still needed to know where LaSalle was going to be. Danny Reilly was her only lead.

All the clothes she kept at Eddie's had been laid out on his bed. She stood looking them over. Nothing was right or even close to being right for the occasion.

"Jordan?"

She turned.

Theresa stood in the doorway, her suitcase sitting at her feet. "I overheard you with the guys. I can help with this if you'll let me."

"What do you have in mind?"

SHE WALKED OUT OF Eddie's bedroom forty-five minutes later. "Okay, posse, let's hit the trail."

Coop, Tank, and Diego turned.

She knew Theresa had done the job well when their eyes bugged and their jaws dropped.

Diego and Tank were mute, but not Coop. "Holy crap, Miss Welsh."

Diego said, "Yeah. What he said."

Theresa walked out behind her and fist-bumped with Jordan. "Looks like we're a success," Jordan said.

Theresa had teased her hair on top and around her face, letting the rest cascade down around her shoulders. It was wild and loose like a gypsy dancer's. Her lips were coated in Theresa's On the Town red lipstick and her eyes were lightly lined with a soft brown and shadowed with a smoky taupe. Mascara brought her lashes out so far she could almost see them when she blinked. She was a little self-conscious. She normally wore only a subtle lip gloss and eye shadow.

The black dress was a slinky-knit, long-sleeved sheath, a little snug and a lot short, since Theresa's 5'5" didn't quite meet Jordan's 5'10". It clung to her curves like Saran Wrap. It was a nice dress, and an LBD was perfect for nearly every occasion.

Thank God her red Jimmy Choos had been in the bottom of Eddie's closet.

Once Theresa had finished, she stood back, chin resting on one fist and said, "Jordan. Even I'd ask you out on a date tonight."

Jordan hoped she was every bit as alluring as Theresa and the crew seemed to think she was. She was determined to keep Danny's attention focused solely on her.

MARTINIS AND IVORIES, DOWNTOWN Phoenix's current *in* spot, had been on Jordan's let's-go-there list for months, but she had wanted to go there with Eddie.

The place was a throwback to the Playboy Club days of the early sixties. The dim ceiling lights cast reflecting halos on the chrome tabletops. Mirrors reflected the fashionable images of the hip, young downtown Phoenix professionals perched on ebony bar stools. The syncopated rhythms of an excellent pianist swirled the open space under the din of conversation and laughter. It smelled like perfume, after-shave and booze. At eleven p.m. the place was in full swing.

Eddie would have loved it.

Back at Eddie's, Tank had buried a tiny microphone in the V-neck of Theresa's black dress. His cheeks flamed and his hands shook. He looked away more than he looked at what he was doing. He must have apologized at least twenty times, while Coop kept offering to take over.

A similarly small in-ear receiver was hidden among the waves and curls of Theresa's creation. Jordan was wired for sound and ready to get down to it.

She walked in and looked around the bar. Diego and Coop were at a table against the far wall. A cocktail waitress in black Spandex capris, red bustier and stilettos was practically lying across their table as she took their order.

Movement at the bar drew her attention. A small crowd parted as Danny Reilly emerged from its center. She had to say he cleaned up well. His black sweater and tight black jeans made him look as deadly as he probably was.

When he saw her, his smile lit up the bar like a searchlight.

"Jordan Welsh." His voice still had that musical quality.

"Mr. Reilly." She tried for a coo.

He lifted her hand to nearly shoulder level and led her across the room like a princess.

He held a chair for her and saw her seated before rounding the table and sitting. One raised finger brought another of the sexy waitresses with a tray bearing two martini glasses.

Danny raised his, Jordan hers. She sipped. A perfect vodka martini. The pianist struck up a jazzy version of "I Saw Her Standing There." Danny leaned on his elbow.

Jordan had been off the market only five or six months since she and Eddie became a couple. How was it possible to forget male-female chitchat in such a short amount of time?

"That's a cute sweater," she said.

He just looked at her.

"No, really," she said. "I really like it."

Danny looked at her like she stepped out of a UFO. "You like it that much, I know where you can get one just like it."

Diego and Coop laughed in her ear. She guessed her sexual banter wasn't up to par.

"Seriously, Jordan? Try complimenting him on the drinks he ordered." Coop's voice was sympathetic, even if he nearly choked on suppressed laughter.

"Excellent martini." She started over.

"Much better," Diego whispered in her ear.

"Well," Danny said, "if Martini's in your name you better make a good one, I say." He raised his glass a second time. "You rock that dress. And those heels … *ai-yai-yai.*"

She crossed her arms and leaned toward him.

It sounded like Diego choked on his drink.

"What a nice thing to say, Danny."

"Careful, Miss Welsh." Coop's voice was hesitant. "I'm getting some static. You could pop the mic out."

She straightened up so fast she nearly knocked her drink over. "Oops."

Danny frowned. "Something wrong?"

"You …" Jordan hurried to say, "you make me nervous." It was the truth. She was nervous as hell.

A lopsided smile lifted one side of Danny's mouth. "Is that a good thing or a bad thing?"

"Nervous?" Diego said.

"Wow. Never had a woman like Miss Welsh tell me I made her nervous," Coop whispered. "Good thing. Right?"

"Shut up," Jordan ordered.

Danny raised his eyebrows.

Jordan's mind raced. "… and kiss me."

"I like the way you operate, Jordan Welsh, and you haven't even asked me about LaSalle yet. Great way to negotiate."

He opened the door, so she walked through, pulling back right as his lips were about to meet hers. "About LaSalle—" she began.

"Uh-uh, pretty lady. Let's not spoil a good thing."

He stood, drew her up and began to sway with her to the tune of "The Sweetest Taboo," nibbling her ear and breathing softly against her neck. Honest to Pete, this guy was his own biggest fan.

And she acknowledged she was a fool to ever believe he'd even give her the time of day unless she gave back exactly what he had in mind. She wouldn't do that, but it wasn't a problem. She had a way around that, and all she had to do was wait for Tank to get back.

Diego and Coop took her at her word and didn't speak for well over half an hour.

Danny kept her busy—drinking, dancing, and being seduced. She must have looked at her watch a dozen times before Tank's voice sounded softly in her ear. "It's done, ma'am. Y'all can call it a night."

She looked across the table at the gorgeous man who had turned and signaled the waitress.

She sighed. Second thoughts assailed her. Maybe this had been the wrong thing to do. Maybe Danny Reilly wasn't such a bad guy after all.

He leaned back in his chair, his eyes on her face. "I've heard a little about Shea Investigations. Your company, right?"

She nodded. Where was he going with this?

"You have a partner, too." He stopped as if trying to recall something. "Eddie Marino? That's his name, isn't it? Eddie Marino's your partner."

She caught her breath.

"I heard he's had some trouble."

She stared at him. How the hell would he know about Eddie if he weren't involved?

What was he playing at? Trying to intimidate her? Did he somehow know about what Tank had been doing? Was this a threat?

Okay. Her blood turned to ice in her veins. He was even

scarier than she thought. Coop had been right about Danny Boy Reilly. Deadly. Dangerous. But they couldn't turn back—the plan was in motion. It was too late.

The look on Danny's face was smug, maybe even calculating. "You think I'm stupid or something, sugar?"

Well, yeah, I was hoping. She didn't answer or even blink.

"I know why you're here. I know you're playing me, but I figure, what the hell? Maybe we can work something out—you and me. I give you something, you give me something back."

Coop's voice rose above the rest of the crowd noise. He was singing, Blondie's "One Way or Another" … sort of. It was way off-key. Jordan turned and ice cold beer splashed over her shoulder and down the front of the dress.

Danny shot to his feet, his voice loud. "Hey, asshole. Watch what you're doing."

Coop leaned over, squinting his bright blue eyes as he peered at her. "Sorry, pretty lady. I'm just … I'm just …."

"Aw, man, look at you." Diego pulled Coop upright and hustled him toward the door, turning back to say, "Lightweight. Whatcha gonna do?"

Jordan sopped up what she could with one of the smallest cocktail napkins she'd ever seen then looked at Danny, who was still riled and glaring after Coop and Diego. He finally sat down and looked across at her. "Want me to go out and teach him some manners?"

She laughed. "No, thanks, Sir Galahad." *Sir Galahad? Right. Danny Reilly is anything and everything but pure of heart.* "I need to drain the puddle of beer in my bra." She stood and picked her bag up off the table. "If you'll excuse me, I'll just …." She lifted her chin toward the far side of the bar, where a neon sign flashed *Babes.*

"Don't keep me waiting long." Was it her imagination or was there an edge to his voice that hadn't been there before?

She nodded, and walked toward the ladies' room until she

was swallowed up by the crowd. Then she headed straight for the front door, exiting right after Diego and Coop.

"Not long at all, Danny Boy. Just forever."

Chapter 33

~

TANK PULLED HER PILOT around to the entrance and she hopped in. Diego and Coop were already in the back.

She turned around to Coop. "It would have been nice if you'd drunk more of your beer before you dumped it on me."

He shrugged. "Didn't want to miss."

She gritted her teeth. "It isn't even my dress. Theresa's not gonna be happy. Throw me that backpack, will you?"

Coop tossed it to her, and she pulled out a pair of jeans, sneakers, and a long-sleeved T-shirt.

After yanking the jeans up over her hips, she crossed her arms, reached for the hem of the dress and pulled it off. When she came up for air all three men were looking out their respective windows. Tank, shy Southern boy that he was, whistled something snappy Jordan didn't quite recognize. She yanked off the tape holding the mic to her breast and tossed it over the seat then shrugged into the T-shirt.

"Let's get out of here," she said.

Tank shifted into gear and pulled out onto Jackson Street then turned right and headed south.

"How'd it go?" Jordan asked.

"Like cake," he answered. "The contents of locker number four-thirty-eight at Blackie's Gym, signed out to one Danny Reilly, are exactly what we thought."

Diego reached over the seat and thumped Tank on the shoulder.

Coop tsk-tsked. "Drug dealers are so freakin' predictable, aren't they? I mean, really? Keeping merchandise in a gym locker? Dude!"

Jordan took out her phone. "I'm calling in the cavalry. Tank, let's head on over there."

Coop sat back. "Thanks for letting me come along, Miss Welsh. There's a lot I can learn from you." He sounded surprised.

Ironic, thought Jordan. Coop's remark made her see what they were doing in a clear, passionless light. If she were honest, this was as much about revenge as anything. But in the end, it was righteous. After all, it wasn't as if she'd planted the drugs in Reilly's locker. Danny Boy Reilly had cooked his own goose.

Tank took another right, then a left. They were down by the tracks and Jordan saw what he had in mind.

"No, Tank. Turn around."

"Miss Jordan, aren't we going after Eddie? We can't just leave him there."

"We're not leaving him. I've made arrangements for Eddie to come home. Tonight. But we can't be part of it. We're going to Blackie's Gym now."

He looked at her.

Nobody said a word. She wasn't even sure the boys were still breathing. "I promise you. It's handled—Eddie's in capable hands."

"Detective Murphy." It was obvious the call woke her up.

"It's Jordan."

"Jordan? What is it? Are you okay?"

"Yes. I'm okay."

"Is it LaSalle?" Ann asked. "Did you get LaSalle?"

"No, but we have a promising lead." She took a deep breath then went on. "A tip on a known accomplice of LaSalle's. It could well lead to information on the coin collection."

Ann yawned. "Hope it's a good one. Do you know what time it is?"

She didn't. Not really. Jordan looked at her watch. Twelve thirty. If it wasn't all over but the shouting, it soon would be.

MUST HAVE BEEN AROUND eleven thirty or later. Maybe. Angel had come back to be his watchdog and Eddie knew from observation the gringo switched out with Angel around eleven or eleven thirty, every twelve hours.

He felt like crap. His head and face throbbed. He'd been hit so many times he'd lost count. Circulation to his hands and feet was cut off thanks to the tight duct tape. He'd lost feeling in them a long time ago.

He was too weak to fight now, so they'd quit dosing him with the drug. Angel called it "sux." Succinylcholine. He'd heard of it. Potent. Surgeons used it to keep patients immobile during procedures. Paralytic, but not sedative. It was perfect if you wanted to beat the crap out of somebody while he was unable to do anything about it and still have the poor sap hurt like hell the whole time.

Speaking of which …. "When do you think LaSalle's coming back here?"

Angel looked up from the comic book but ignored the question.

Eddie tried to shift in the chair and take some of the pressure off his back and hips. He'd been thinking things through and had come up with a plan that might just get him out of this. If he told LaSalle he'd lead him to where the coins were hidden, at least he'd be mobile.

The only regret he had about the way things were going to end was, of course, Jordan. They'd hardly even had time to get to know each other very well, although he still felt like he knew her better than anyone else on the face of the planet.

Jordan. The fire in her eyes flashed through his mind. He could almost hear her laughing at some silly thing he'd said. That was the best reason he could think of to put on the ridiculous Jersey Shore goomba act. It made Jordan laugh.

God, how he wished he'd had more time with her.

She'd be okay. Jordan Welsh always landed upright, just like the Weebles Gina used to play with when she was little.

He'd never let Jordan know just how far gone he was, never let her see he needed her a thousand times more than she needed him. He would have liked to have the chance to set a few things straight with her.

The service door slammed. Eddie's head jerked up, his heart in his throat. He hadn't heard it open, but it banged shut like a gunshot. LaSalle was back. Time was up. *Do or die.*

His worst nightmare strolled across the big empty space like he was window-shopping. He stopped in front of Eddie, slapping an airline ticket jacket against his palm. "My ride out of here. I can't hang around much longer. Since I'm such a swell guy, I'm gonna give you one more chance before I punch your ticket."

Tony pulled out those damned leather gloves and slipped them on.

Eddie watched him do it, every nerve in his body on alert. Showtime. "I got a proposition for you, Tony. Untie me, and I'll take you to where the coin collection is stashed."

He rubbed his knuckles against his palm. "You mean you're not going to give me even a few knocks? I mean, I think I deserve at least a few shots at you."

Eddie shook his head. "But I'm going to give you what you want."

Tony looked almost disappointed. "Okay. But why now?"

Eddie just looked up at him.

"Oh, sure," Tony said. "The girl, right? You're playing hero, trying to save the girl. Ain't that just too, too noble of you."

"You *are* still interested in the gold. Right? I mean, if you don't want me to give 'em up—"

"No. I'm interested. It's too late for me to stay here—the Mexicans already have me on their hit list—but I'm not stupid enough to turn down a few million bucks toward my retirement. Still, if you think I'm turning you loose …."

Eddie shrugged. "Those are my terms. What do you have to lose? Hell, you'll be with me. Bring Angel along. He's three times my size. He can pick me up and throw me against the wall with one hand. I'm in no shape to walk away, not before you're ready for me to, that is." *And I know your plan never included my walking away.*

LaSalle frowned and zeroed in on Eddie like a rattler before a strike. Eddie found he was holding his breath as Tony began pacing in front of him. *Do it, Tony. Do it. Sure, it's a trick, but it's your only shot. Hell, it's my only shot.*

After what seemed like an hour or two, but was probably only a couple of minutes, Tony stopped pacing, took off the gloves, and jerked his head at Angel, who walked around behind Eddie and cut the duct tape off his arms.

When he yanked it off, Eddie hissed.

After he was free, Angel grabbed him under one arm and jerked him out of the chair.

Eddie's legs cramped and collapsed. Angel held on and Tony grabbed the other side. They turned toward the door.

Tony's head jerked up as the overhead door engaged and began to crank up. Two men dropped to the pavement and rolled under it ninja-style, followed by a half dozen just like them. Eddie recognized a few of the men. They sprang to their feet, automatic weapons leveled at Angel and Tony.

Tony and Angel let go of Eddie. He hit the concrete floor with a grunt. It hurt like hell.

He raised his head as the door lifted, and Anthony Vercelli strode into the warehouse like Patton marching into Sicily.

Tony was smart enough to stay where he was and not even twitch. He raised his hands. Angel followed suit.

Vercelli's face was in shadow, but his body language radiated rage. Without stopping or hesitating, he drew his arm across his body and backhanded Tony across the face.

"I trusted you, you son of a bitch." Vercelli didn't look away. "You okay, Eddie?"

Eddie wanted to sing, but instead said, "No, sir. Not okay. Not even close."

"Stay still just a couple more minutes," Vercelli said. "Something I need to address then we'll get you out of here."

"No problem, Mr. V." Relief so powerful he couldn't contain it surged through Eddie.

One of Vercelli's men took Angel aside, patted him down, and led him outside. Vercelli was totally focused on LaSalle. "You have some things to answer for, Tony," Vercelli said.

Tony began to shake.

Eddie didn't blame him, not one bit. Vercelli's bad side was damn scary at best.

"Not just for Eddie. The Mexican cartel has been hot and heavy on my ass. I understand I have you to thank. It seems they had the impression it was me stealing their product, not you." Vercelli went on. "And now this ugliness with Eddie …. Tsk, tsk."

"And Muggs," Eddie ground out. "Don't forget about Muggs."

Vercelli nodded. "Muggs is on your dance card, too."

Eddie had heard Vercelli make similar statements. It wasn't good, and apparently Tony LaSalle knew it too.

"Anything I can do about this, Mr. V?" Tony asked.

Vercelli shook his head. "What do you think?"

Tony shrugged. "No way I'm going down without a fight."

He reached into his waistband, yanked out a big automatic pistol and raised it to draw a bead on Anthony Vercelli.

As Tony's arm came up in a burst of gunfire, Eddie grabbed his ankles and yanked his feet out from under him. Tony came down hard, his head snapped back, and his gun clattered to the floor as he collapsed on top of Eddie. Eddie couldn't do anything but try not to suffocate as a half dozen gun barrels descended toward Tony's head.

"Hold your fire," Vercelli ordered. "Leon, get that piece of garbage off of Eddie."

Chapter 34

BLACKIE'S GYM WAS DARK when Jordan and the crew arrived.

They waited in the parking lot and watched as two Phoenix PD blue-and-whites pulled up, along with a Ford Explorer. The cherry topper on its roof made it obvious it was a police vehicle as well. Ann and Neil got out of the Explorer. Jordan and the crew joined them.

"Impound?" Jordan asked, indicating the Ford.

Neil made a face. "Yeah. We couldn't find anything better. No sports cars tonight."

"Sorry to get you out of bed, Detective Thompson," Jordan said. "You look terrible. You probably could have used the rest."

"Very funny, Welsh," he said. "You drag me out in the middle of the night, you better have some damn good info. Who's this secret informant of yours, anyway?"

She shrugged. "Really? If I tell you who it is, it's not much of a secret, is it?"

Ann, beside her, spoke into her ear. "But you are going to reveal your source. Right, Jordan?"

"My source? We're looking for this LaSalle guy, and we have

feelers out all over the place. On the streets, on the inside, everywhere. Let's just say one of those feelers came back that this Reilly guy and Tony LaSalle are dealing drugs together. And we're confident enough of the information provided to follow up on it. Who knows, maybe it's connected to the Dahlonega theft."

"I don't like the way you operate," Neil said. "You or that Marino guy either. Something off about him, if you ask me."

Jordan put out her arm to bar the way as both Tank and Diego moved in on Neil.

The detective's eyes widened in alarm.

"What was that, Neil?" Jordan asked. "I don't think I heard you clearly. Were you casting aspersions on my partner?"

He grumbled and moved away.

Jordan turned to Tank and Diego. "Where's Coop?"

"Taking a nap," Diego said. "Past his bedtime."

Jordan laid her hands on each of their shoulders. "Why don't you join him? I think I have this one covered."

A bald, muscle-bound fifty-something man-ape arrived in a Chevy pickup.

He spoke to the Phoenix officers, unlocked the door to the gym and went inside.

All the lights were on in Blackie's Gym by the time everyone went in. Neil showed Blackie the warrant while Ann took the lead. One of the Phoenix cops followed them with a lock cutter.

Jordan breathed a sigh of relief when she saw Blackie. He hadn't been present when she and Tank talked to Reilly there that morning.

"Men's locker room?" Ann asked.

Blackie led them.

Jordan followed along as if she didn't know the way on her own.

As she remembered, the concrete floor was pitted and cracked, paint chipping off the lockers. It looked clean, but the smell of sweat and gym shoes hung in the air while the heavy humidity assaulted them all. The curls Theresa worked on for so long collapsed out of Jordan's hair.

"Four-thirty-eight?" Blackie stopped. "Here ya go."

They all stood back while the cop moved in, snapped the lock off, and stepped aside.

Ann and Neil looked at each other then at Jordan.

"Well, let's see how good your secret informant is." Sarcasm had always been Neil's specialty, but tonight he really rubbed Jordan the wrong way.

She slanted Ann a look and spoke beside her ear. "How can you stand working with this miserable jerk?"

Ann smiled. "He lets me drive."

Neil reached for the handle and opened the locker.

Even though Jordan knew exactly what was inside, she held her breath. Tank had told her every item in the locker—from the can of Axe deodorant, to the illegally modified Colt .38 automatic handgun, and a hundred-foils of black tar heroin in a baggie like Jordan used for leftovers.

This might have been the first time in a long while that Detective Neil Thompson smiled—not just smiled but laughed out loud. "What do you think about that? Didn't find the gold coins like we came for, but now we have this Danny Boy as a consolation prize."

"How you like me now, Neil?" Jordan broke into song and dance. "I'm awesome. I'm awesome. I'm awesome."

"Smartass," Neil said.

Ann interrupted. "Don't pay any attention to Detective Thompson. Nothing like a white girl with rhythm and a good CI."

"So, does that mean the boys and I can tag along on the bust?"

Neil opened his mouth. The look on his face said he was about to object when Ann said, "Sure. The more the merrier."

JORDAN HURRIED BACK TO the Pilot, got in and buckled up.

All four sat quietly for a moment, their combined breathing sounding like bellows.

Finally Jordan asked, "Did you do it?"

Tank's whispered voice was oddly amplified in the quiet interior. "Yes'm," he said. "I took the bag of coins to LaSalle's place. Stashed 'em in a metal storage shed in the backyard behind a couple of cans of paint, covered the bag with a tarp. Cops oughta find them easy—even old Detective Neil Thompson."

"Let's find a phone booth then and make the call."

They drove around for almost half an hour before finding a public phone that actually worked. Coop got out to call the Scottsdale PD anonymously and tip them off as to where the coins were hidden.

Jordan watched him walk across the street to the convenience store. An oversized camouflage hoodie pulled low over his face would guard his identity from any security cameras.

She thought back to her childhood days in Lake Forest, Illinois. On the days Jordan and her friends went to hang out at the mall or the movies, her mother always gave her two extra quarters. "Here, Jordie, in case you need to call me." Good luck with that these days. Public phones were about as rare as personal privacy. The stress she'd been under was probably what caused this moment of nostalgia. She wondered what mothers did these days. Ah, never mind. Every kid had a smartphone. Mothers didn't need their kids to tell them where they were; all they had to do was track them.

Coop returned to the car, got in the back and shut the door. "Just call me stool pigeon. Coo-coo."

THEY DROVE ACROSS TOWN and dropped Coop at Eddie's place.

"Check on Mama Rose, Coop, but stay loose in case we need you." She pulled her phone.

"Calling to check on Eddie?" Tank asked.

She nodded. Sofia's voicemail picked up. "Hi, Sofia here.

Sorry I missed your call. I'll call you back between exciting adventures."

"Really? Figures," Jordan said. "It's Jordan. Call me, Miss Excitement."

Jordan was beside herself. A word from Vercelli or Sofia would go a long way toward remedying her worry over Eddie. She had opted to call Sofia rather than the man himself because having Vercelli on speed dial could bring up difficult questions if anyone checked her phone.

"How long until they get the warrant for Reilly?" Diego asked.

"Don't know for sure. Neil's so hot to make an arrest, he'll probably go to the judge's house and pull him out of bed."

"You want to head over to Reilly's?" Tank asked.

"Might as well," Jordan said.

The cellphone rang. Jordan answered before the second ring. "Sofia!"

"They got him."

A thousand-pound load lifted from her shoulders. Eddie. Eddie was free. "How is he?"

"Messed up, but he's going to be okay. I'm at the hospital with him now. Poppy called and said I should come stay with him."

I'm supposed to be with him. Not her. "Which hospital?"

"All Saints Hospital. Because he was beat up so bad and Poppy's guys are, you know, who they are, they couldn't bring him in the usual way. They left him outside the ER."

"Did they even stop or just push him out on the roll?"

"They made sure he was okay and waited around until someone came outside and brought him in. They're taking good care of him. I'm with him now."

I wish she'd stop reminding me of that. "Did he ask for me? Does he understand why I'm not there?"

She would have given anything to be there when Eddie woke. Her face should be the first thing he saw.

Sofia seemed to understand her distress. "He's drugged, Jordan, for the time being anyway. Just come as soon as you can." Her voice was sympathetic.

"I'm going to call his mother," Jordan said. "Thanks, Sofia. Stay with him as long as you can. He needs someone there who cares about him."

"Jordan?"

"Hmm?"

"He'll know why you're not the one he woke up to," Sofia said. "If anyone will understand why you couldn't be connected to the rescue, it's Eddie. Don't worry."

Jordan turned toward the guys. She took a deep, ragged breath. No tears in front of the men. "Eddie's fine. He's going to be fine. Vercelli got to him in time."

"Thank God. You don't know how hard it was to stand back and wait for someone else to go get him," Diego said.

"Eddie's like our brother," Tank added.

"Do you guys think I don't how hard it was to stand back and let someone else take control?" Jordan's tone might have been a little sharp, but she wasn't in the mood to take it back. "I explained all this to you already. None of us could be part of this rescue or even appear to have knowledge it was going down. If someone got killed, Eddie wouldn't want you to be connected."

"Or you," Diego said.

"Or me."

"But Vercelli got the job done," Tank said.

"He was the only one I could trust to get Eddie out safe. And the old crook did it."

Chapter 35

⁓

Danny's residence was located on Central Avenue on a lush estate. Big palm trees lined the street. Thick privet bushes were tall enough to conceal anyone coming or going from the house. Probably why he bought the place. Drug dealers needed privacy. Made it all the harder to conduct surveillance.

Tank parked the Pilot across the street and down a few houses.

Jordan's phone sounded "Bad Boys."

"Ann, what's your ETA?" Jordan asked.

"We're pulling up right behind you."

Jordan opened the car door, got out, and walked back to the Ford. Detective Neil Thompson was probably still cranky about having to drive such a piece of crap car while making his big arrest, although Jordan thought it fit him. If you asked her, he'd look stupid in a drug dealer's Maserati or Ferrari. "You get the warrant?"

Ann waved a folded piece of paper. "Hey, you're talking to Scottsdale's finest. Of course we got it. Neil practically helped the judge get dressed so he could authorize it."

A look passed between Jordan, Tank, and Diego. She had called it.

Neil Thompson wasn't known for his brilliant case solving. This one would be a real feather in his cap.

"Way to go, Neil," she said, ignoring the bird finger he lifted in her direction. "What's the plan? You going in on foot?"

"No, we're dropping down the chimney," Neil sniped. "What did you think? We were bringing in choppers and para jumpers?"

Jordan shrugged. "One never knows when you're on the case, Sherlock."

By the time Phoenix and Scottsdale PD had staged the area with a ridiculous amount of tanks, MRAPs, and enough heavy artillery to overcome a small city, the heavy-hitter SWAT guys from Phoenix and several tactical cops from Scottsdale had surrounded the estate. Tank and Diego hung back by the mobile command post. Ann and Jordan hunkered inside the base unit with the tactical coordinator.

Jordan waited for the go signal with Ann. "You guys always throw such a big party for one measly drug dealer?"

Ann shrugged. "You can never be sure what you'll find inside. Could be ten heavily armed mercenaries waiting for us in there."

The SWAT leader's voice was audible in the coordinator's headset, but the words were indistinguishable to Jordan.

"Okay. Go." The coordinator turned to Ann and nodded.

Ann took a deep breath. "They're on their way in."

Jordan stepped outside. Tank and Diego turned. "It's a go," she said.

Her heart beat faster. Her breaths came in jerky, shallow bursts. This bust could go down easy or go down hard. When this many cops with this many guns and this high a level of motivation moved in, it usually went down the hard way.

They waited, expecting the chaos to begin any second—

staccato volleys of gunfire, flash bangs, rapid bursts of radio transmissions as status and orders were exchanged.

But minutes passed, a half hour. And still nothing. None of the shock and awe that went along with the usual SWAT raid.

Instead, the unit door opened. Ann stepped out and said, "It was a simple lock. They just snapped it and walked in. Danny Reilly's in the bedroom. Let's go get him."

The four joined Neil at the curb and they walked up the long curving driveway to the house, which sat back off the road at least half the length of a football field. Winter lawn, beds of flowers, fountains, statuary. Jordan's mother would have thought she'd died and gone to English garden heaven.

The house was a sprawling, low-slung territorial with a Mission tile roof. Light came from a few of the windows.

The only sound was the persistent, high-pitched yip of a small dog somewhere nearby.

Two SPD tactical officers stood at the door.

Ann, Neil, Jordan, Tank, and Diego went in.

No one was in the living room except a Phoenix PD sergeant holding a pissed-off rust-colored Pomeranian who growled and spit and snarled like he was going to take off the cop's head.

The sergeant restrained the dog against his chest. It squirmed and twisted, but the cop held on.

Jordan walked up to the sergeant, took hold of the Pomeranian's collar and made it look at her. "Calm down for crying out loud," she said softly. The pup yipped once more then looked straight at Jordan with a thank-God-you've-come expression. Jordan took it from the cop and tucked it under her arm. Poor thing. Probably scared to death, although you'd never know from the sound of it.

"Jordan?" Ann's voice carried from down the hall.

Jordan discovered half the assault force, as well as Ann, Neil, Tank, and Diego all standing around a king-size bed. In the middle of the bed, Danny Reilly sat upright with his hands behind his head. Beside him a voluptuous blonde cringed, the sheet pulled up under her chin. The blonde was one of the sexy servers from Martinis and Ivories.

Danny stared at Jordan when she walked in, his expression giving away nothing.

Ann moved forward. "Okay, Reilly. Up. I bet you know the drill. Danny Reilly, you're under arrest for possession and suspected sale and distribution of heroin." Then she began her Miranda spiel.

"Oh, Danny," the blonde squeaked.

Danny Reilly patted her on the arm but didn't move further. His eyes found Jordan's before he spoke. "Like they say, I have the right to remain silent. I want to call my lawyer."

"Let's go, Romeo," Neil said.

Danny slid out from under the sheet and stood, naked except for his black silk boxers.

Using his most impressive detective swagger, Neil went to the side of the bed, picked up the tight jeans Jordan had seen Reilly in at the nightclub. Neil tossed them at Danny.

Jordan walked out of the bedroom, scratching the dog behind the ear.

"Hey, in case you were gonna ask, go ahead and take the damn dog!" Danny's voice followed her down the hall. "Two o' you deserve each other. Stupid thing pees on the rug."

SHE STOOD OUTSIDE ON the front steps. The air was cool. A light breeze stirred her hair. The little dog licked her hand and snuggled against her. *Not exactly the animal I pictured for a guy like Danny. An Irish Wolfhound, maybe.*

Ann walked up beside her.

"Nice job, Detective Murphy," Jordan said.

"Busy night." Ann reached over to pet the dog. "We're heading over to Tony LaSalle's place."

"Oh." Jordan tried to sound innocent. "Do you think he's there?"

"Maybe, but that's not why we're going. We received an

anonymous call that the Dahlonega collection might have been hidden there. We searched his place once already, but it's worth a second look, especially if LaSalle got nervous."

"No word on LaSalle himself?"

"Not yet," Ann said, "but we'll get that sleaze. Think you want to come with …?"

Jordan seemed to give the question the appropriate amount of thought before answering, "No, better not. It's been a really long day. You've got a lot going on tonight, too. You don't need me tagging along everywhere. It makes Neil cranky."

"Everything makes Neil cranky." The detective looked down at the little dog. "You taking the pooch with you?"

"I was thinking about it. Is that a problem?"

"If we need his testimony, I'll give you a call." Ann put her arm around Jordan's shoulders. "Thanks for your help tonight."

"We didn't get LaSalle, but it wasn't a total loss."

"Are you kidding, Jordan? Tonight was a win, and we'll find LaSalle and the coins, too."

Jordan watched her friend walk back to the Explorer.

Tank and Diego stopped beside her. "Y'all want to go see how the boss is doing?" Tank asked.

Diego said, "Bet he's in a really bad mood, unless they have some good-looking nurses taking care of him."

"Watch it, or I'll sic this vicious dog on you," Jordan warned.

She stepped down off the porch. "Let's get over there. Call Coop to come pick up this pooch and take him back to Eddie's place. Theresa can keep an eye on him."

Chapter 36

～

ALL SAINTS HOSPITAL WAS quiet at seven thirty Sunday morning when Jordan, Diego, and Tank finally arrived.

Eddie's room was on the fourth floor.

Jordan caught her breath when she walked in.

Not only was Eddie out cold, but he looked terrible, like someone the grim reaper had forgotten to pick up—right forearm bandaged, left hand ditto, left cheek swollen, right eye discolored and swollen, lower lip split. The nurse on duty mentioned two cracked ribs to be cautiously babied for six to eight weeks. Her eyes burned. *Oh my God, Eddie. What the hell did they do to you?*

Sofia sat next to him. No makeup, hair like a haystack. She looked exhausted.

"Jordan," Sofia turned and saw them, then stood and backed away, "I'm so glad you're here. Come sit down with him."

Jordan looked over at her. "Any change?"

Sofia nodded. "He woke up for a few minutes about a half hour ago. He seemed to know where he was, who I was." She paused. "He asked about you."

Jordan reached out to touch him, but pulled back. Where

could she lay her hand and not hurt him? He seemed to be one massive bruise. Instead she leaned over and gently placed a kiss on his left eyelid—the Indiana Jones scenario. He moaned, and she was looking into his beautiful brown eyes, Eddie's eyes, yet not. A haze dulled the fire she was so used to seeing there.

"Hey, babe," he slurred, "where you been? You smell like beer. I could use one right about now."

"Heavy date tonight," she teased. "What was I supposed to do? You were tied up."

He laughed, sort of. She could tell it hurt his ribs by the way he twisted to protect himself.

Diego and Tank pushed away from the wall and moved over to the far side of the bed. "Boss," Diego said.

"Brother, you are a sight," Tank drawled.

"Good to see you guys, too." Eddie shifted in the bed again.

"Eddie," Sofia said. "How are you doing? Are you clear-headed enough to understand if I tell you something?"

He turned his head slowly toward her. His eyes did seem a bit more focused.

"My dad called a couple of hours ago." She took a step closer to the bed and lowered her voice. "LaSalle's dead."

No one spoke, waiting for her to continue.

Sofia began, "Yeah, he was out cold when they loaded him into the trunk, but they overestimated how hard he was hit. He must have come to, and when they were stopped at a light, he popped the trunk from the inside and rolled out of the car."

Jordan was confused. "But I thought you said he was—"

"Dead." She smiled. "He is. Stupid bastard took two steps away from the car and got flattened by a semi." She snorted. It wasn't attractive at all. "It was a McDonald's truck. Talk about your all-beef patties."

Jordan stared at her, appalled that someone could take such glee in another's death—even if that someone were the Devil himself. Maybe Sofia was her father's daughter after all.

Sofia sang. "I'm lovin' it."

Tank laughed.

Diego somehow managed to hold it back, but Jordan could tell it was hard by how red his face was.

Only Eddie didn't seem to find it funny. And Jordan? Jordan could only send a silent prayer for forgiveness. *Thank God the son of a bitch is dead.*

"I WANTED TO TELL you in person. I know you need closure on the case," Ann said, in full detective mode.

When Ann called and asked to see her, Jordan left the hospital and drove to the station. Now she sat across from her friend trying to look surprised and interested as Ann related the news of Tony LaSalle's untimely demise.

"The traffic cams picked it up. It was an old Mercedes four-door, reported stolen yesterday from a location in Central Scottsdale. On the footage, the trunk lid popped open. LaSalle jumped out, hit the ground running—or tried to, anyway. He only took a step or two before the semi flattened him. I'll never be able to order fries again without thinking of that sleazebag. The Benz took off. We found it a couple of miles away, wiped clean. We figure the cartel went after him, like maybe something went wrong with one of the drug deals LaSalle and Reilly were in on together."

She sat looking at Jordan, seeming to expect a response. Evidently Jordan didn't come up with one fast enough to suit Detective Murphy. "You don't seem all that surprised to hear about this, Jordan. You don't happen to know anything about it, do you?"

"Me?" Jordan said. Too bad she hadn't paid more attention in her high school drama class. "Ann, I was with you, remember?"

Ann nodded slowly. "Yeah," she said, "you were."

Something in her friend's eyes—disappointment, maybe even hurt—dumped a load of guilt at Jordan's feet. When your business partner and lover had a history with the mob, and your best friend was a cop, being straight with them both wasn't always in the cards. Better if Ann never knew she was the biggest part of Jordan being able to deny knowledge of Vercelli's actions.

Chapter 37

~

MONDAY MORNING AT TEN thirty sharp, Jordan pulled the Pilot up to the curb at the hospital's main entrance.

Eddie sat in a wheelchair on the sidewalk, scowling.

Before she stopped the car, he was up and out of the chair, opening the door, and climbing in.

"What the hell took you so long?"

Oookay. "Sorry. Didn't think it was 'so long.' "

"I felt like a chump sitting in the damn wheelchair. Nothing wrong with my legs."

She struggled to keep a straight face. "You're right."

He offered a wave to the candy striper, who smiled and waved back before she turned the wheelchair and headed back into the hospital through the automatic sliding doors.

"I'm right?" he asked. "What's that supposed to mean?"

Tough as beef jerky, her Eddie Marino, but he hadn't been able to hide the wince as he stepped up into the car. No wonder he was grumpy. She went with it. "It means I took a long time getting here, there's nothing wrong with your legs, and you felt like a chump sitting in the wheelchair."

He stared at her a long minute. Then he relaxed and smiled. "Yeah, sure. Let's blow this joint."

MAMA ROSE AND DIEGO met them in the parking garage of Eddie's building.

Rose ran to Eddie but the arms she circled around him were tender and soft. "My boy! I was so worried."

He looked at Diego over her head.

Diego's gaze met Eddie's. "Couldn't keep her from coming to meet you. She was crazy to see you, boss."

All four took the elevator up to Eddie's place. He looked tired and shaky. Jordan hoped his family had the good sense not to plan a party. No matter what he said or pretended, he obviously wasn't up to it.

Theresa was waiting out in the hallway with Coop. When she saw him, she ran to Eddie and wrapped herself around him. He wasn't quick enough to hold her off and winced. "T, sweetie, let go. You're killing me."

"Oops. Sorry. Baby brother, oh man, was I ever worried about you. Me and Mama, we couldn't sleep, couldn't eat, and couldn't think. It really sucked."

"Thanks for coming out to be with Mama." He put his arm around her shoulder and guided her back into the condo. "I'm sure you were a great comfort to her."

The look he gave Jordan over Theresa's head said he didn't think anything of the sort.

Once inside, Eddie excused himself to take a hot shower. Rose and Theresa headed to the kitchen—Italian women to the bone.

Jordan waited a few minutes then went down the hall to Eddie's bedroom.

It was at least twenty minutes before the shower shut off, and Eddie walked from the bathroom naked.

He was getting around better, almost like he always did—strong, athletic, feral, but slower than usual. His beautiful body was marred; his arms, legs, and torso were covered in purple and green bruises. There were scrapes on his knees and hands and a few round, angry-looking red marks that might even have been burns.

Tears stung her eyes, but she didn't offer sympathy. He wouldn't want it.

She quickly stripped down to her bra and panties and crossed to the bed. Lifting one corner of the duvet, she threw it back before she lay down and rolled onto her side, patting the empty spot beside her.

He smiled and started toward her.

"Don't get any funny ideas, Mr. Marino. This will strictly be resting."

"No?" He sat then swung his legs up under the covers. He couldn't repress a soft grunt. "Not even a little cuddle time?" He lay down beside her. By the way he twisted to find a comfortable spot, she knew it would be some time before he was back to normal.

Jordan rose up on one elbow and studied his poor bruised face. The swelling had gone down, but the remnants of the cruelty dealt him courtesy of Tony LaSalle were there in his eyes.

"Cuddle time?" she said. "Well, maybe just a little."

"Anything you want to tell me?"

The third degree was inevitable. Eddie always needed to know all the details. She told him everything, even about the date night with Danny Reilly.

Eddie listened intently, and when she was finished, he let out a long sigh. "A drug dealer? You crossed a drug dealer? On your own? Jordan—"

"I wasn't on my own. Not really. The crew, they were with me."

He nodded. "Yeah, and I'll deal with them later." He took a good long look at her and shook his head. "Jesus, Jordan, you scare the crap out of me."

"Scared? Why? You know I can take care of myself."

He stared into her eyes for several minutes then his lids began to droop, and he drifted off.

He slept for over an hour. She lay quietly beside him the entire time, watching him, still unable to believe that God had really answered her prayers and delivered him back to her.

VERCELLI'S NEW RIGHT HAND man, Leon, answered the door and stood back while they entered. "It'll just be a minute," he said. "Good to see you, Eddie."

The door to Vercelli's office opened, and two Hispanic men wearing silk cabana shirts and designer-label slacks came out. Leon led them back to the front door.

They avoided eye contact with Eddie and Jordan.

Anthony Vercelli sat behind his gorgeous antique desk, smoking a really smelly cigar. Jordan tried not to make a face. His silver hair was slicked back, not the way he usually wore it. His tanned face was smooth and clean-shaven. The light blue silk sport coat he wore over a tropical print shirt must have run him twelve or fifteen hundred dollars. Even Mary Welsh would have been impressed.

Vercelli stood when they walked in, came around the desk and embraced Eddie.

He acknowledged Jordan with a smile and a nod. They sat in large wingback chairs.

"*Eduardo*," Vercelli rounded behind his desk and sat. "You're on the mend I see."

"I came to pay my respects and express my gratitude for what you did, Mr. Vercelli. I'm in your debt."

Vercelli shook his head and leaned back. "No, son. We're even. I set the record straight with those two gentlemen from the cartel. Once Reilly was out of the picture," he smiled at Jordan, "courtesy of some Machiavellian maneuvers by the lovely Miss Welsh, a couple of his guys looking for an employment opportunity revealed where he stashed the rest of his goods. I returned a fortune in black tar heroin to the cartel—a particularly substandard grade if I'm any judge. But thanks to you, I don't have to worry about a drug war anymore. And you saved my life in the warehouse. It looks like I owe you."

Eddie looked relieved, and Jordan knew why. Owing a debt to a man like Vercelli could weigh heavily on a man.

ON WEDNESDAY AN UPBEAT article came out in the paper regarding the recovery of the Golden Dream Dahlonega Coin Collection and its return to the Arizona Heritage Museum. The article praised the Scottsdale Police Department, who had worked in concert with the Phoenix PD and Shea Investigations and Security of Scottsdale. Local TV news vans were parked outside the agency, soliciting Jordan and Eddie to appear on the nightly news on several of the local stations.

The Abromowitz sisters and the Arizona Heritage Museum board planned to host a champagne reception at the museum in their honor.

The phone was ringing off the hook with new business. Gina and Coop fielded all aspects of this activity like slick Hollywood agents.

Eddie was back to working fulltime and growing stronger every day. He was healing on the inside as well.

Chapter 38

~

IT WAS SATURDAY, ALMOST two weeks since Eddie came home from the hospital, the day of Mama Rose's wedding.

Ivory satin ribbons and white lilies and roses were everywhere in the chapel of St. Aidan's Parish. The wedding decorations only served to enhance the graceful arches of the beautiful and serene, old Spanish style, white stucco building. Angels celebrating the Virgin birth exploded in rich color over the panels of stained glass behind the altar. As always, the chapel was cool and dim and comforting. Eddie could see why it was Jordan's favorite place of worship.

Mama Rose was lovely in a silky, beaded lilac gown with a long-sleeved jacket over it. Mary Welsh's beautician had spent the morning with Mama, weaving baby's breath and purple orchids through her hair.

She stood with Eddie outside the double doors in the foyer, waiting for the string quartet Mary hired to strike up the song she and Mark chose as their own personal wedding march.

"Look at all the people," she said. "I can't believe how many showed up. Where did they all come from?"

Eddie shrugged. "Some are friends of mine and Gina's, and

Mary said a lot of her friends were excited to come. They're all gaga over your celebrity author status, Mama."

Rose giggled. After a quiet moment, she said in a sly voice, "Did you see how beautiful Jordan looked?"

Had he seen her? He could hardly take his eyes off her. She nearly knocked him out in a lapis blue, long-sleeved sheath that fit her like a second skin. She even dug out the four inch Jimmy Choos she loved so much. Every click of those stiletto heels drove him crazy. "She's a beautiful woman."

"You think she looks gorgeous today, just imagine how beautiful she'd be in a wedding gown." His mother's expression was wily.

"Really, Mama? This is supposed to be all about you today. You can nag me about marrying Jordan tomorrow."

But even he had to admit the idea of seeing Jordan in a wedding gown wasn't as intimidating as it had been a few months ago.

"I'm just sayin', son. You and Jordan belong together. Any fool can see it. You can't deny love, Eddie."

What could he say? Mama's words of wisdom always rang true. But he didn't have to think about it right now. The string quartet rang out the first chords of Pharrell Williams' "Happy," and Mama Rose took his hand and started to shake and shimmy up the center aisle to where Mark and Theresa danced in place, their smiles huge.

Happy? Yes, he spun Mama Rose under his arm and pretended to catch the kiss Jordan blew him.

Jean Steffens and Sally J. Smith

SALLY J. SMITH AND **Jean Steffens** are partners in crime— crime writing, that is. They live in Scottsdale, Arizona, an awesome place for eight months out of the year, an inferno the other four. They write bloody murder, flirty romance, and wicked humor all in one package. When they aren't putting their heads together over a manuscript, they haunt movie theaters, malls, and great restaurants.

For more information, go to www.smithandsteffens.com.

41301074R00145

Made in the USA
Lexington, KY
08 May 2015